THUNDER RANCH

Tuck just shook his head and drove the ATV slowly and quietly back down the grade.

The jaguar came out of the small opening in the rock face of the butte and stretched; he was hungry and thought only of his next kill. Suddenly, he threw up his head and sampled the strong westerly wind as it brought traces of the men's scent to his nostrils. On the other side of the gully that separated him from the road, he saw the ATV moving slowly as Tuck tried to get into a position to surprise the cat. He couldn't know that the jaguar had decided on him for his next meal.

Tuck brought the Polaris to a complete stop and killed the idling engine. He would have to cross a very thick portion of the gully and get to the cat quickly if he wanted to get home by dark. Tuck tightened his Kevlar leggings and started the walk down into the dense brush with all of his senses on alert. Not only did he have to keep an eye pealed for rattlesnakes, but there were other things besides the jaguar that could hurt him in here.

The jaguar had Tuck's scent now and made his fast-paced stalk to within fifty yards of his position without being seen. It would lie in wait until the human had passed him, and then rush in to seize him from behind and crush his head between his powerful jaws. Tuck was moving slowly past the jaguar at an angle that had shortened the distance between them to thirty yards. The cat could taste the blood in his mouth and his every nerve was focused on making this kill.

ISBN 978-0-9862487-2-6

Published by Purple Sage Entertainment, Odessa, Texas

Printed in the United States of America on acid-free paper.

purplesageentertainment.com

W.W. Brock

brock@wwbrock.com

http://www.wwbrock.com

THUNDER RANCH

W.W. Brock

W.W. Brock

Dedication

I would like to dedicate this book to my wife, the love of my life. Without her support and encouragement, I would not have started writing.

W.W. Brock

PROLOGUE

The aging Cessna 206 touched down quietly on the barren, grass-covered runway of the Rancho de Truenos, Thunder Ranch, near Sheffield, Texas. Situated miles from the nearest interstate and accessible only by several miles of dirt road, the runway activity was also hidden from prying eyes by its location below the towering buttes to the North and South, and the dark of the night. The flight had originated in Mexico, and coincided with a 'Bonsai' swarm of illegals charging across the border checkpoint at Eagle Pass, Texas en masse. Flying low to avoid radar and with its running lights off, the six-passenger plane skirted the tops of the high bluffs, staying close to the valley floors, and running by radar.

When it arrived at the GPS coordinates for the little used ranch runway, the pilot keyed his mike in a prearranged sequence, and a confederate on the ground answered by turning on the headlights of an SUV that had parked strategically so that it could illuminate the landing area.

The pilot cut power to the single engine aircraft and settled it on to the hard packed ground, stopping just short of the SUV. Four men with packs and armed with military grade AK-47s quickly disembarked the plane and loaded into the SUV, which drove away into the night with its lights off. The plane taxied back to a take off position and quickly departed, the pilot executing the plan to fly the plane back to the south, and then climb to an altitude that would expose it to radar. He would then set an easterly course, put the plane on autopilot, and bail out over his pick up area.

Fifty miles south of the ranch, just as the pilot eased back on the controls to begin his climb over a towering rock wall, the Continental engine sputtered twice, caught again for a split second, and then died. The official cause of the crash, which wasn't discovered until two weeks later, was pilot error, but the real cause were the two gallons of distilled water that had been poured into the wing tanks on the last fuel stop, freezing in the fuel lines, and then soaking into the ground after the crash.

Miguel Sanchez had been the foreman for the Rancho de Truenos, Thunder Ranch, so named because of the thunder echoing off of the high buttes and hills that surrounded the ranch during the West Texas storm season, for the past five years before it sold suddenly to a gringo rancher from Midland, Texas a month ago. Today would be his last day on the ranch, and probably his most profitable. He had heard the small plane as it revved the engine for take off, and now he hurried on his ATV to the only dirt path that served the runway area for the prearranged meeting.

The SUV stopped where Miguel stood, and the driver's window opened just long enough for the driver to toss a thick envelope into Miguel's eagerly waiting hands.

"Gracias Amigo!" Miguel shouted to the taillights of the moving SUV, as he looked at the ten thousand dollars in crisp new one hundred dollar bills that he now held in his hands, "Mucho Gracias!"

He hurried back to the trailer that had served as the bunkhouse for him and his men before the sale, and took his bag with a small amount of clothes to the old Chevrolet truck that he brought to the ranch with him five years before. Everything else that he had accumulated over the past few years he left behind. Miguel was going home.

CHAPTER 1

"Mr. Tucker, I need to spcak to you in the hallway please," The doctor said to Tuck as he finished examining Hanna and removed his gloves.

"Yes sir," Tuck answered as he leaned over and kissed his wife on her forehead, "I'll be back in a minute Hon," Hanna just gave him a small smile and squeezed his hand.

Tuck left the small birthing room behind the doctor who waited in the hallway. Speaking in low tones so as not to be overheard in the room, he said to Tuck, "Mr. Tucker, due to the trauma that your wife suffered early in this pregnancy, I'm afraid that we may need to deliver by caesarean. The bones in her pelvic girdle just aren't strong enough for a normal delivery."

Tuck thought about this for a minute while the doctor waited patiently for his decision although Hanna was already dilated eight centimeters, and almost ready to deliver, "I need to ask Hanna, doctor. She was adamant about natural birth so it has to be a joint decision."

"I understand, but you need to hurry. I'm going to prep an operating room," The doctor replied.

Tuck went back into the room and took Hanna's hand, "Hanna, we need to talk about the delivery."

Hanna was drained from the pain of her labor, and her voice seemed strained and weak, "Is something wrong, Michael? Please tell me the baby is alright."

"The baby is fine, Hon, but the doctor says that your pelvis is not strong enough for a natural delivery. He is prepping a room for a caesarean," Tuck responded calmly.

"I don't want a caesarean, I want some Demerol!" Hanna's voice went from weak to insistent as her fingernails dug into Tuck's forearm.

"I know, I know," Tuck tried to reassure her as her gently pulled his arm away from the crab-like grasp of his wife who had just entered the transition phase of her delivery, "But we need to think about the baby, Hanna. If something goes wrong, and he doesn't get delivered right, it could affect his brain permanently."

"I want some Demerol right now or I am going home!" Hanna struggled to rise up out of the delivery bed.

The nurse who had been standing patiently at the foot of the bed, moved quickly to Hanna's other side with a syringe held steadily in her hand.

"Of course you can have some Demerol Mrs. Tucker. Let me take care of that right now," She said with a soft smile as she gave Hanna an injection for her pain.

The nurse looked at Tuck and nodded toward the doorway as a signal to follow her out side.

"Mr. Tucker, I know that this is not the way that you envisioned your wife bringing your son into the world, but she is in no condition to do this thing naturally. I've already taken care of the matter so you need to man up. Go back in there and hold her hand while I get a gurney. We are going to delivery this baby in about five minutes!" With that announcement, she hurried off down the corridor toward the nurse's station, leaving a stunned Michael Tucker standing in the hallway.

Tuck returned to the room to find Hanna very groggy from the sedation, "Michael, I want this little boy to grow up just like his daddy," She said slowly, her words slurring slightly as she sank ever deeper into sleep.

"I know, Love. I know," Tuck gently reassured her as he waited for the nurse and the gurney. He couldn't help but feel sad that Hanna wouldn't get the chance at a natural delivery, but that concern would have to wait.

The door to the room swung open suddenly as the nurse returned with the gurney and a helper. They positioned it next to the bed and using the sheets, pulled Hanna onto the gurney, and whisked her out of the door with Tuck bringing up the rear. Down the corridor to the operating room, they went at a fast walk. The delivery nurse took Hanna in while the other nurse showed Tuck the change room and handed him a set of scrubs.

"Hurry and change Mr. Tucker, that baby is not going to wait much longer," She said with a smile before leaving the room and closing the door behind her.

Tuck felt like he was all thumbs as he tried to hurry. His forehead was sweaty and his hands shook, as they had never done in his whole life. Before he had time to think about that, the door was opened again and the doctor stuck his head in.

"Time's up Mr. Tucker. We need to get this delivery rolling!" he said with a smile as he motioned for Tuck to join him in the operating room.

"Now I want you to stand at the head of the operating table, Mr. Tucker. We've got the sheets up so that you can't see the procedure. Just talk gently to your wife, and we will have a baby out here in just a couple of minutes," The nurse said as she explained to Tuck what was going to happen.

Tuck's legs suddenly felt like jelly, and his mouth was as dry as if he had swallowed a teaspoon of West Texas dust. There was a ringing in his ears, and it seemed as if spots were swimming before his eyes. He heard the nurse as if from a fog.

"Mr. Tucker, are you alright?" she asked with concern.

Tuck mumbled, "I'm fine ma'am," However, he wasn't sure about that. He kept hearing, "Man it up Mr. Tucker!" in his head as if on a playback loop.

The next few minutes dragged by as Tuck gently stroked Hanna's moist hair and forehead with a damp cloth. He was trying not to pass out by not looking at all in the direction where the doctor was cutting into his wife's belly. Suddenly he was snapped back to reality by the cry of a baby as the doctor gently lifted the child from its mother's womb and slapped it on the behind. Just before the room went black Tuck heard, "Well, I'll be. It's a girl!"

CHAPTER 2

"This is never going to get old!" Henry Albright exclaimed loudly between gales of laughter.

John Post had just finished retelling the story of Tuck's delivery room experience for the third time, embellishing the story each time with just a little more 'flavor' as is sometimes the tradition among great story tellers. Tuck just sat across the table shaking his head while the men had a good bit of humor at his expense.

"You know guys; it wasn't at all like it sounds. I just got a little light headed and had to sit down for a minute. That's all," Tuck made a feeble attempt to protest the roasting that John and Hanna's Uncle Henry were giving him.

"And I suppose that's where that knot on your head came from…just sitting down for a bit?" Henry dug in just a little bit as he and John broke into another fit of laughter.

"While you men are enjoying yourselves, I'm going to go see how the ladies are getting along," Tuck answered in frustration as he got up and walked in to the living room of the Post's house where Mary Louis Post, Kathryn Albright, Hanna's stepmother, and Hanna sat with the new arrival.

"Michael, everyone wants to know the name that we've picked for the baby," Hanna said as she handed the little package to Tuck with a smile. The little girl had been such a surprise to them that a name had not even been discussed until after the delivery. As they were joined by Henry and John from the kitchen, Hanna made the announcement with a smile and tears in her eyes.

"We have decided to name our little girl 'Emily Albright Tucker'!" Hanna declared to the gathering, "We wanted to keep the Albright name alive in memory of Daddy. I think that would have made him happy."

The rest of the afternoon was filled with tears and laughter as the events of the past few months were remembered and then put behind them, but not forgotten. Harry Albright would have wanted it that way.

Finally, John, Henry, and Tuck went outside for a walk around the yard, and a look at the new geese in the pond.

"Tuck, I haven't had the time to tell you, but that mess over in Big Joe's pond has been cleaned up. As a matter of fact, I took Big Joe and Myrtle both out of there because of the liability of having alligators that size in a water hole with all of these 'Oilies' traipsing around the ranch."

John was referring to the two big alligators that had been placed in the water tanks almost thirty years before, "We buried all of the other stuff where nobody will run across it in this life time."

Where did you put the 'gators?' Tuck asked.

"Let's just say that they disappeared and let it go at that," John said with a smile. He started to add something, but his cell phone rang before he could finish.

"Hello," He answered, "Yep, he's right here with me now. He might be. I'll sure tell him."

John hung up the phone and turned to Tuck, "I just got a call from Luke Moffett, that tall fella that you met a couple of weeks ago at the gun shop. He says there is a rancher down near Sheffield that is looking for somebody to manage his deer herd, and kind of watch over the place. What do you think?"

Tuck thought about it for a minute before replying, "I think I would like to talk to him about it. Did you get the number?"

"We're going to meet him for breakfast in the morning. Luke already set everything up," John replied with a grin.

"Tuck, it looks like lady luck is smiling down on you," Henry chimed in, "This is right down your alley, and it would be remote enough to keep you out of trouble."

"Well, Harry told me not to trust in luck, but I do believe that this is something that would be considered a divine appointment. What does the terrain look like down there? Is it as flat as this ranch?" Tuck asked as he looked over the miles of flat land covered in mesquite shrub, cactus, and sparse grass.

"No, that area is pretty rough with lots of buttes, gullies, and hills. The grass is good down there though, they've had plenty of rain. I know this ranch that Luke is talking about, it is a beautiful place well off the highway. The Mexicans that used to own it raised Spanish fighting bulls and Andalusia horses down there," John replied, "You'll find out all about it in the morning."

Tuck's phone rang, so he stepped away from the group to answer and saw that it was FBI Special Agent Anthony Morris calling form Myrtle Beach, South Carolina.

"Hello Agent Morris" Tuck answered the phone.

"Hello Tuck. I just want to call and congratulate the new father. Good news travels fast," Agent Morris replied.

"Thank you, sir. I'll be sure to pass the warm wishes on to Hanna," Tuck was still a little puzzled at the call.

"There is one more thing, Tuck. Joel Biggs is in your area looking for clues to the whereabouts of Agent Kensey. His car was found abandoned not to far from your location, and there is some concern that he may be getting ready to cause you some trouble," Morris finished.

"I haven't seen anything of the man," Tuck answered truthfully, "but I hope that you find him. I don't need anymore of that trouble following us. Tell Joel to call me and stop by. We are having a little get together to celebrate the baby, and he would certainly be welcome," Tuck said.

"I'll do it immediately, Tuck. You take care of yourself, and let me know if you see anything suspicious regarding Kensey."

"Yes sir, I certainly will keep my eyes open for trouble from that guy. Tell Joel to call me, and I'll drive out to the main gate and let him in," Tuck hung up the phone.

"Who was that, Tuck?" Henry asked.

"Special Agent Morris, he wanted to tell me that Agent Joel Biggs was in Goldsmith looking for Kensey. I invited Joel out for the party," Tuck replied.

"The more the merrier!" exclaimed John Post, "I saved about twenty pounds of alligator tail to fry up for this cookout. It should make that fellow feel right at home. Now let's get everything set up."

"Have you cooked alligator before, John?" Tuck asked.

"I've cooked everything from catfish to mountain lion, and I suspect that 'gator won't be much different than rattlesnake. It'll be fine," John said with a laugh. Henry and Tuck just exchanged glances and rolled their eyes.

Twenty minutes later, Tuck's cell phone rang with the expected call from Joel Biggs, "Hello Tuck, this is Joel. Anthony Morris told me to give a call and come see you. Is now a good time?"

Tuck knew that putting off the meeting would seem suspicious to Joel, so he invited him over, "Hello Joel, It is certainly good to hear from you! Come on over and join us for a new baby celebration cookout. I'll meet you at the gate."

"That sounds good, Tuck. I'll be there in about ten minutes," Joel accepted the invitation and ended the call.

The celebration was in full swing with about twenty of John and Mary Louise's closest friends from the West Texas Cowboy Church taking turns congratulating Hanna and Tuck on the new baby girl. The West Texas sunset lit the ribbons of

high clouds with a hue of red and orange that made the sky look like it was on fire.

"Tuck, can we go outside and talk for a minute?" Joel Biggs asked.

"Sure," Tuck responded as he headed for the door.

John and a few of the men were cleaning up the cooker so Tuck led Joel over to the fence that separated the yard from the pond.

"Tuck, I'm concerned about Kinsey's car being found so close to here, and I don't think that you're safe as long as that maniac is loose," Joel was blunt and to the point.

"Joel, I can assure you that Kensey is no threat to me or my family, so stop worrying," Tuck responded with a smile, although he knew that Joel would not let this go.

"How can you be certain about that, Tuck?" Joel asked with a good bit of suspicion showing in his look.

Tuck decided to keep Joel in the dark so he simply replied, "I just am."

"Another thing that we are confused about is why George Withers would steal your boat instead of killing you and Hanna. It just doesn't make sense," Joel skipped over any more questions about Douglas Kensey and switched to George Withers.

"I wasn't aware that he had, Joel. Did you find him or the boat?" Tuck asked innocently.

Joel gave a laugh and then answered, "I was just trolling there. No, we didn't find any remains of Mr. Withers, although we were able to determine that it was your boat that was run down by that container vessel. You're really not going to tell me anything about that are you, Tuck?"

"I don't see that it would serve a purpose now, Joel. Besides, I just want whoever Withers worked for to forget all about us, if that is possible," Tuck replied.

"He worked for us, Tuck! I'm hoping that Withers had been freelancing with the attempted hit on Hanna, but I'm afraid that is not going to be the case. Sooner or later, something is going to stir up these people again, and then it will start all over. You can never get away from an organization as large as the government once it decides that you are a threat," Joel finished.

"Do you think that it is the government that is after us?" Tuck asked in amazement.

"Not the whole government, of course, but someone very powerful that controls enough of it to be able to do as he or she pleases without recourse," Joel replied, "You need to blend in somewhere and not make any ripples. I'm saying this as a friend because you are still in danger as long as there is a chance that they perceive that you might be a threat."

"Now you're making me regret not going to Honduras with Bob and Abby. Well, I'm not running, Joel. Harry told me one time that unless God ordained it, no weapon formed against me would prosper. Tomorrow, I am talking to a man about a job managing a deer herd on a secluded range down south of here. I don't see how that could get me into any trouble with anybody," Tuck replied.

"Just take care of yourself, Tuck. You know that Anthony Morris and I will have your back as much as possible. I've got a report to write. Tell John thanks for the hospitality, and say good-bye to Hanna for me," Joel shook Tuck's hand and walked to his car. Tuck just stood looking across the miles of mesquite to the horizon that was on fire with the last rays of the setting sun, his thoughts on Hanna, Emily, and Joel's words of warning.

CHAPTER 3

To fourteen-year-old Emanuel Hernandez, the opportunity to help with the shearing of almost one-hundred head of sheep on the Cannon Ranch came as a gift from God. His mother had struggled to raise the family of six boys and girls since her husband had visited relatives in Mexico and disappeared five long years before, and her son's earnings from his cowboy activities went a long way to keep food on the family table. Emanuel, or Manny as the ranch hands called him, drew the task of watching the ewes the night of the shearing. The next day's activities would include making certain that they had their shots before being turned loose to pasture. Tonight they were all corralled, and it fell to Manny and another young man the responsibility to guard them from any predators that might seek an easy meal of mutton, but the odds of that happening were so remote that Manny had left his old Remington .243 in the front seat of the beat up Chevrolet truck that was parked behind the corral.

By eleven o'clock, the small fire that the boys had made earlier in the evening had dwindled down to coals, and Manny's partner was snoring in his bedroll, waiting for his turn to stand watch. Manny's eyes had grown heavy, and he was about to nod off, so he decided to walk around the corral in an effort to stay awake. As he turned the corner on the enclosure, a shadow moving silently out of place with the mesquite and cactus suddenly appeared right in front of him. In the darkness that was illuminated only by a three-quarter moon, a very large black cat sailed effortlessly over the six foot fence that encircled the corral, grabbed a one hundred and fifty pound bleating ewe in its powerful jaws, and bounded just as effortlessly back over the fence, landing right in front of the startled and frightened Manny Hernandez! It stopped about five yards away, turned its head toward Manny, and fixed a particularly evil glare on the boy while emitting a deep growl of warning. The panther then melted into the mesquite with the still struggling ewe grasped firmly in its mouth, leaving Manny weak with fear, and not quite certain what he had just witnessed. With his legs still feeling like they would buckle under him, Manny turned around and ran toward his truck to retrieve the rifle while calling to his partner to wake up, but it was too late, the big cat had melted into the shadows of the mesquite and cactus. The boys spent the rest of the evening until daybreak feeding the fire and their imagination with speculations about what animal had taken the sheep so easily out of the corral.

Thirty years later, Manny Hernandez still woke drenched in sweat as the demon cat of his nightmares fixed eyes that resembled burning coals on his face as it slowly advanced toward where he stood frozen in fear.

"Manny, Manny, wake up, you are having that dream again," Maria Hernandez shook her husband gently awake.

Manny slowly opened his eyes and looked at his wife. His heart was beating wildly in his chest, and sweat was beading on his forehead, "Maria, thank God that you woke me up. I believe that the demon cat was going to get me this time."

"Oh Manny, you need to talk to someone about this dream, maybe a priest or a psychiatrist," Maria said softly as she stroked her husband's head.

"You talk like I am crazy, Maria. I'm just having nightmares about the panther that I saw when I was a boy. I don't need a psychiatrist, and I sure don't want a priest!" Manny responded with a little anger in his voice.

"Don't get all defensive, my husband. I just think that you need to confront this thing before you have a heart attack or something, although if you did, I would get the business, and maybe a new young man that didn't snore so loudly," Maria responded with a sleepy laugh as she turned over to go back to sleep.

Manny just grunted as he turned to snuggle his wife's back. She was right of course, he needed some help, but from where would it come from?

CHAPTER 4

Luke Moffet, a tall Texan in his mid sixties, made the introductions the next morning at the Wagon Wheel Restaurant, just before they seated themselves at the table with a gray bearded man of medium height and build that appeared to be in his late sixties. At first glance, Otis Jamieson appeared to be just another older man used to a life of hard work, and still in good physical shape, but Tuck saw something in his eyes that he had noticed before in men that were either combat hardened or had a law enforcement background. He made a mental note to ask Otis about his past if the opportunity presented itself.

"Otis, this is Michael Tucker, John Post, and Henry Albright," Luke made the introductions as the men shook hands in turn and seated themselves around the table.

After the introductions were made, and the breakfast was ordered, Otis Jamieson wasted no time in finding out what Tuck knew about deer herd management.

"Well sir, The South Carolina DNR wasn't so much interested in the number of bucks in a given area, but more about the condition of the herd overall. There were times when we had to increase the number of anterless tags to keep the number of deer on any given forage area within the bounds of their food supply. I have studied different models of herd management for increasing antler size and also for increasing the buck to doe ratio," Tuck filled Otis in on his basic knowledge of the management issue.

"I've got fourteen thousand acres down there, Tuck, with about eight hundred deer that we could count from a helicopter. What would be your recommendation for that herd?" Otis asked.

"To start, I would try to determine the ratio of bucks to does. With a herd that size, a good ratio would probably be one buck for every two and one half does, give or take. We don't know what the mortality rate is among the herd either. Although I would suspect that it is fairly high or you would be overrun with deer in a couple of years with high levels of starvation in the months of reduced forage," Tuck pulled from every conversation that he had engaged in the past two years on the subject of herd management.

"I do feed during the month or so leading up to hunting season and we have a few good heads in the herd. The biggest problem is that the people that owned the ranch before killed everything indiscriminately, even the fawns. How do we rebuild the herd from that?" was the next question he asked Tuck.

"I probably would try to get an accurate ratio of bucks to does first, and then, if the buck side was around one to four, I would restrict the taking of any bucks except for culling for about two years. I would also try to arrange with the wildlife folks for permits to reduce the number of does in the herd until they were at the prescribed level. By the end of two years, you should see an improvement in the buck to doe ration, which will mean more bucks sighted during the rut, and see some larger heads being grown. Of course that doesn't take into account any predatory animals eating the herd either," Tuck finished, knowing that Texas was well known for having big cougars in the trans-Pecos range.

Otis smiled and extended his hand to Tuck, "I think you are the man that I am looking for. Let's get to our breakfast before it gets cold, and I'll see you at the ranch tomorrow for a tour. What do you think?"

"I think this is a great opportunity, and I thank you for letting me have a crack at it, Mr. Jamieson," Tuck replied.

The talk around the table then turned to the latest bad news coming out of Washington, how America needed a change of leadership, and the falling price of oil before finishing their third or fourth cup of coffee, eggs and bacon, and heading for the parking lot.

"Tuck, I'll see you at about eight-thirty or nine in the morning," Otis said as he shook Tuck's hand again.

"Yes sir, I'll be there," Tuck replied although he wasn't sure where 'there' was.

"Luke will make sure that you don't get lost, and my name is Otis. Stop calling me sir!" With that, he climbed into his truck and left before Tuck could say, "Yes Sir!"

"Well Tuck, it looks as if this is going to work out for you and Hanna," Henry said as they bid good-bye to Luke and got into Tuck's old Buick for the ride back to the ranch, "I'm headed home tomorrow, but I want you to call me if there is anything that you kids need."

"Henry, we are in pretty good shape financially with the boat settlement and all. I think that once Hanna is healed from the delivery, we are going to be just fine. I am a little concerned after talking to Joel that the troubles with the government aren't over, but at least they are quiet right now," Tuck replied.

"Just remember that the people that we ran afoul of are not very forgiving, and you stuck your finger pretty deep into their eye, Tuck. I'm proud of you for that. I just wish that I could find the bastard that killed Harry," Henry spoke bitterly.

Tuck kept his silence on the matter while they were in the car because he was very certain others might be listening. He made up his mind to tell Henry about the run-in with Douglas Kensey when they arrived at the ranch.

"I've got something to show you before we get back," Tuck said as he turned off of the well-worn roadway onto a narrow trail that ran across the mesquite and cactus covered ranch toward the windmill that he jogged to every morning. Once there, Tuck parked the car about one hundred yards from the tank. As they got out, he took his cell phone out of his pocket and tossed it in the front seat while motioning for Henry to do the same.

As they walked toward the cement water tank, Tuck said to Henry, "I thought that you might like to know that the man responsible for Harry's murder died out here," Tuck said in a matter-of-fact way.

Henry was silent for a minute while they stood gazing at the pond below the tank, and then he asked quietly, "Did you kill him, Tuck?"

"No, he got himself eaten by a big alligator while he was trying to kill me! I know that God must have had something to do with that. What are the odds of coming all of the way out here to the desert, and then get eaten by an alligator right in the middle of all this cactus?" Tuck kind of chuckled at the thought, but he had not thought it was funny at the time.

Henry just stared at Tuck for a long minute, and then said, "Harry used to say that God works in mysterious ways, Tuck. I feel better now that you've told me this. It's as if a weight has been lifted off of me. Of course, we'll probably have to wait for years before this can be told, but what a campfire story it will make! Hey, was that 'gator tail that John fixed last night from that alligator?" Henry asked as he pointed toward the pond.

"I have a suspicion that it was," Tuck replied with a chuckle.

Both men were laughing at the unspoken thought that Joel had eaten some of the evidence in the disappearance of Douglas Kinsey.

"You have certainly made my day, Michael Tucker!" Henry exclaimed as they got back into the car and returned to the ranch house.

Kathryn met them at the door of the little bunk house and spoke in a hushed tone, "Keep it down guys, Hanna and Emily are taking a nap. How did it go, Tuck, Did you take the job?"

Tuck answered excitedly, "I guess I did. Luke and I are going down in the morning for a tour of the ranch, and I will probably be gone for most of the day. The prospect of losing ourselves on a secluded ranch certainly seems exciting, doesn't it?"

"I suppose it does Michael, but remember Hanna's condition. She and the baby need to rest for a week or so before starting another adventure. Besides, I am going to be here for another week to look after her and my granddaughter before I head down to Honduras to see Abigail Pike. They've insisted that I come down, and everything is going smoothly back in Myrtle Beach," Kathryn replied.

"I have an idea," Henry interjected, "Since I am leaving tomorrow and won't be seeing you all again for a while, let's go out to dinner tonight, my treat. I have a taste for some Mexican food while I am down here,"

"That sounds good Henry, but what about Hanna?" Tuck asked.

"What about Hanna, what?" came a small voice from the bedroom.

"Hi Hon, Uncle Henry wanted to go out tonight for Mexican. I didn't want to leave you here by yourself," Tuck answered.

"For goodness' sake Michael, having a baby doesn't make a woman an invalid!" Hanna called out with a laugh in her voice, "Of course I'm going!"

"It's settled then," Henry replied, "Pick a place. I'm going to go find John and look around a bit."

"Our girl is a strong woman Michael," Kathryn stated as she shooed him toward the bedroom to see the baby.

Tuck just gave her a grin.

CHAPTER 5

Tuck met Luke the next morning at the Wagon Wheel for a quick breakfast before the hour-long ride down to the Thunder Ranch. Tuck thought it was interesting that the only way into the ranch was on a roughly three mile long dirt road that cut across another ranch property, so after a rough drive across the adjoining ranch and through several cattle gates, Tuck and Luke were greeted at the Thunder Ranch by Otis.

"Good morning men are you ready to take a little ride around the ranch?" he asked jovially as they shook hands all around.

"Yes sir," Tuck replied for both of them, "This is certainly a big place that you've got here. I'm looking forward to seeing as much as I can."

"Well, you can't see it all in one day, but you'll have a lot of time to look it over if you decide to help me out with my deer herd," Otis replied.

With that, he led the way to a Polaris Ranger that was sitting with its twin near the old ranch house. For the next three hours, they toured the ranch and stopped to look for sign at every water tank and feeder location that they came to. As they rounded a bend in the dirt track that they were on, Tuck spotted the carcass of a yearling heifer lying just off of the path.

"Look over there Otis!" He exclaimed while pointing in the direction of the body.

"It looks like coyotes might have killed this one," Luke ventured.

Otis replied as he inspected the kill, "I would suspect a cougar over coyotes Luke. That heifer was coming downhill, and the attacker had to have been above her. Look at the way her front legs are broken. Something heavy rode her down before killing her."

As they examined the carcass, which had been eaten almost entirely except for the skin and the head, Tuck noticed something interesting.

"I don't think that this was a cougar either. Look at the four puncture wounds in the top of her head. It's almost like whatever killed her, crushed her skull, and punctured her brain with its teeth," He observed.

Otis got up suddenly and looked nervously around the mesquite, cactus, and large rocks that surrounded the area that they were in, "Let's get back in the ATV and ease out of here. There is only one animal that kills like that, and I don't want to be standing here with just a light shotgun if it shows up."

Tuck and Luke exchanged a brief glance as they walked back to the Polaris. When they were underway again, Tuck leaned over to Otis, "What kind of animal does that?"

"Jaguar!" was the reply, "If they are black they call them panthers. They aren't supposed to be around here anymore, but since the President re-authorized them to bring these exotics back in the area from Mexico, we've heard stories. The jaguar runs about one-fifty to three hundred pounds, and has the strongest jaw of any of the three big cats. They don't act like the cougar either and have almost no fear of man when they get cornered. I've heard that whatever they fix their eyes on they attack. Whether that's true or not, I don't know. I do know that even if they are protected, I don't want them on my ranch killing my stock, so act accordingly."

Tuck was well aware of the problems that the government had caused by openly approving the reintroduction of predators back into the environments where they had been driven out years before. He also knew of the insidious reason that they had done it, and how dangerous it was to cross those responsible. As with everything that the government was involved in, the issues were layers deeper than whatever might appear to be happening on the surface.

The rest of the day was spent riding around the big ranch and viewing the scenery that it offered. When they returned to the ranch house, Otis asked, “Well, what do you think?”

“Well, it is a lot to take in, what exactly do you want me to do?” Tuck answered.

“I’d like for you to implement a program to manage that deer herd to get more visible bucks like we talked about, and I would also like you to act as my warden out here to protect the property from an poachers or trespassers. That would entail working with the local sheriff and the wildlife department. We’ll clean up the old ranch foreman’s trailer for you and your wife to live in, and we can work out a generous salary package. Interested?” Otis asked with a grin as he stretched out his hand.

“More than interested, you’ve got yourself a warden!” Tuck exclaimed with a grin as he shook the offered hand to seal the deal.

“Great, let’s go in the house and get a bite to eat. I want you to meet my wife Julia. By the way, next week we are leaving for an Alaskan cruise, and we will be gone for around a month. As soon as we agree on the salary, I’ll cut you a check for the next month, and you can start immediately. How does that sound?” Otis asked.

“That sounds good to me, sir,” was Tuck’s response.

“Great let’s go get something to eat,” He replied as the three men walked to the house.

The rest of the afternoon passed quickly and soon Tuck was on the way back to Odessa with Luke. They discussed the day’s activity and Tuck picked the older man’s brain for more information about the ranch, and about his background.

For the next hour, Tuck was spell bound by the stories Luke told about growing up on the ranches that his father managed from New Mexico to Texas, his military service in Viet Nam, and his life as it changed from being a cowboy to being a husband, father, and businessman in the oil patch.

"Had you ever heard much of the Thunder Ranch Luke?" Tuck asked him after he finished his personal narrative.

"Well, there were always reports of strange things going on there when the Mexican's owned the property," Luke replied to answer Tuck's question, "I know that they used to have small planes flying in to that dirt runway at the very early hours of the morning. You could hear them on the other ranches. It seems odd that they took off and left all of the live stock and rolling stock behind doesn't it?"

What did you think about the monkey story?" Tuck asked, "Do you think it might still be out there?"

"Might be he would find his way down in one of the gullies and live there," Luke replied, "but I don't think he would survive very long. Maybe you can catch him if he is still around."

"I wish that we had seen the last of those fighting bulls that is in there. I can't imagine having to dodge a hundred of those things. Did you see the size of that arena? It must have been one hundred feet across and at least eight feet high!" Tuck rambled on about the ranch and Luke filled him in on as much as he knew about the place until they got back to Odessa. Luke dropped Tuck off at the Wagon Wheel to pick up his car.

"Luke thanks for taking the time today. I really appreciate it.' Tuck said as he shook Luke's hand.

"Glad to get out of the house for the day Tuck. If I can help you anymore, just call me. I'd be glad to go back down if you need me to," Luke was being truthful since he missed the cowboy days and the way that he had grown up when his father managed some of the bigger ranches.

"Let's plan on it Luke. Maybe we can hunt that Jaguar on the QT. What do you think?" Tuck asked.

"Just give me a call; I'm sure that Mary would like to get me out from under foot for a couple of days," Luke replied with a big smile before driving off.

Tuck's mind was running at ninety miles an hour as he processed the day's activities. He would have to get a kit together and get back down here by himself until Hanna could come down. Now would probably be the time to buy a decent truck also.

CHAPTER 6

Manny Hernandez woke to the smell of coffee brewing and knew that he had over slept. He quickly got out of bed and dressed before heading into the kitchen where Maria had a big breakfast waiting for him.

"Good morning Manny. After last night I thought it might be good for you to sleep in a little bit," Maria said as she hugged him and gave him a kiss on the cheek.

"Today isn't a good day for me to be late Maria. The men aren't exactly self-starters you know, and I have a big job down on the Rancho de Truenos that will take several days," Manny replied.

"Nonsense!" Maria exclaimed, "You have built this business up by hard work, and you have the right to sit here with me and eat a good breakfast, I insist."

Manny knew that he couldn't argue with Maria and win, especially when she could cook like she did, so he sat down at the table.

"Isn't that ranch near where you saw the devil cat?" Maria asked while Manny ate.

"It adjoins the ranch that I used to work on, but it is several miles from where that cat was. Besides, he has been dead for a long time," Manny replied hoping that it was true, "There is a new owner there now, and I have to talk to him about the work we are doing around one of the tank batteries."

Maria waited until her husband was finished eating, and then gave him a big hug before ushering him out of the kitchen with a pat on the butt, "Have a good day Manny. I'll be at the shop doing paperwork today, so call if you need anything down there."

"I will, but don't expect me home until after dark," Manny replied as he walked to his Ford F-350. His mind was on the dream from last night, and being reminded that he would be near where the cat of his dreams had lived was not the way that he wanted the day to start.

Tuck was at the entry gate to the ranch early and had brought a stout stick along to secure the 'bump' gates that he had to open while he drove the old Buick through them. Common practice was to hit the gate with the cowcatcher on the front bumper of a truck with just enough force for it to swing open and then it would close behind the vehicle as it went through. Tuck was wary about trying that with the car so he got out and propped each of the gates open in turn until he had arrived at the ranch house.

Otis was working outside when Tuck pulled up and walked over to the station wagon to greet him, "Good morning Tuck," he said as he shook Tuck's hand, "You are going to need a truck for this job," Otis commented, as he looked the Buick over.

"I'm thinking of buying a truck now that we are here. There really hasn't been much time what with all of the things that have happened since we arrived," Tuck replied.

"Unless you just want one, you don't need to spend the money. I'm going to furnish you with a truck so that you can haul supplies in and out of the ranch. Consider it a perk of the job," Otis told him, "Now let's take a look around here, and I'll show you the foreman's house that I told you about. I have to meet with a fellow that is doing repairs on one of the pump jacks and the tank batteries on the other end of the ranch, so we'll head over there in about an hour."

The trailer that had served as the foreman's house was run down a bit and needed a good cleaning, but Tuck thought that it would do for Hanna. He hoped it would anyway.

"I know that it doesn't look very inviting right now," Otis remarked, "but since we are leaving for a month, you and your wife can use the ranch house until the contractors fix that one up. They'll get started on it next week."

"I appreciate that, and I'm sure it will be fine," Tuck replied, "Tell me about that arena. Did they actually fight bulls in there?"

"I'm sure that they did, and from the looks of the observation box over there, I believe they flew in guests to watch them also. Those fellows trained the bulls to be man killers so be careful of the one that is still loose on the ranch, and don't make eye contact with him. We are going to take him out soon, but he could still hurt someone," he answered, "Have you got a good pair of snake boots? We have some big rattlesnakes here, and if you get bit, it is a long way back to the house."

"I have some boots in the car that I bought last year," Tuck replied, "I wish that I could've found some made in the USA boots, but that proved next to impossible."

"Well down here in Texas, we have boot makers that can make anything that you want. When you get ready for another pair, just let me know," Otis replied with a smile, "Let's go check on those oil men, and see what they are planning."

They fired up one of the Polaris Rangers and drove across the ranch to meet Manny Hernandez and his crew. Otis took the long way around showing Tuck various places of interest including one large pond surrounded by old oak, mesquite, cactus, and cottonwoods, and the area where a small mule deer herd ranged before driving up to the equipment that Manny and his men were unloading on one of the access roads.

After the introductions were made, Otis walked the job with Manny and told him exactly how he wanted the area to look after they had finished. When they returned to the ATV, he told Manny about Tuck's new role as range manager and warden.

"So Tuck, what do you think of this country?" Manny asked.

"It is certainly pretty in a different way from the swamp lands that I'm used to," Tuck answered.

"You know, I remember that you were on television a while back. It was something about a big cougar over in South Carolina," Manny said.

Tuck replied, "I'm trying to put that all behind now. We came out here to get a fresh start, but I think that is odd to leave an area where everyone was in denial about cougars and come to a place where they are accepted as a menace to the livestock and not protected. The funny thing is that we found a heifer killed yesterday that didn't appear to have been killed by a cougar. From the way that her head was crushed, Otis thinks she was killed by a jaguar."

At the news of the possible jaguar attack, Manny's face took on an ashen look, and his legs almost buckled.

"Are you all right? You look like you've seen a ghost," Tuck asked in alarm as he grabbed the other man's arm to steady him.

Manny had suddenly broken out in a cold sweat and his normally dark complexion became a pasty yellow-brown. He turned to one of the front loaders that was sitting behind them and sat down on the trailer.

"Panthera…devil cat," He muttered under his breath. Then as he slowly regained control, "When I was young I had one of these come right up to me and look me in the eye not to far from this place. It was black as the night, and took a big ewe that we had sheared right out of an enclosure with no effort. Last night I had a dream about this cat again, and now you are telling me that there is one around here. What are you going to do about it?"

Otis replied, "Tuck is the warden here so it is up to him how he wants to handle the jaguar. I just don't want it killing anymore of my cattle."

"I'm not up to speed on jaguar hunting, but they are on the endangered species list, so that could pose a problem unless it was attacking someone. Let me look around for a couple of weeks and see if I can find where its range is, then I'll make some plans to remove it," Tuck responded.

"I would like to be included in the hunt, if you decide to go that way, Tuck" Manny said as he wiped the sweat from his forehead, "I think seeing this animal dead would stop my nightmares, besides, I am a good shot from any distance."

Tuck shook his hand, "Consider yourself included, Manny. It was a pleasure to meet you."

Manny handed Tuck his business card, and then Otis and Tuck returned to the ranch house to discuss the terms of Tuck's employment.

CHAPTER 7

It had been almost three years since the jaguar had left his native habitat in the sub-tropical clime of southern Mexico and started his odyssey north that would bring him eventually through the Big Bend Park corridor and out into the rugged country of South Texas. Prey wasn't a problem since the area close to the border was a habitat for many mammals that the jaguar fed on including an occasional hapless illegal that had wondered away from the rest of the pack and gotten lost. Some had been abandoned by the human coyotes that had taken their money and possessions before leaving them with no water or food for the arduous trek into the vast hostile desert areas.

Today, the big jaguar lay hidden in the dense cover afforded by the thicket of oak and mesquite shrub that covered the high bank of the large pond. His black coat showed the old scars that resulted from an attempt to take one of the Mexican fighting bulls that until recently had roamed the mesquite covered plains and gullies of the Thunder Ranch. Now the panther, as his black state was called, slept in the late morning after taking a large buck that had come to the corn feeder near the water hole. Before feeding on the deer, the panther dragged his kill into the thick brush where he started by tearing into the animal close to the neck and eating the heart and lungs, and after feeding, retreated a short distance away to protect it from interlopers until he needed to feed again.

The sound of the Polaris Ranger broke the quiet of the late morning and woke the panther from his sleep. Instantly alert, the cat watched from his cover as Otis and Tuck stopped the ATV directly across the pond from his location, and then got out to look briefly at the tracks on the edge of the pond, and at the feeder itself. With his muscles tense, the cat thought of retreat, but the men quickly boarded the ATV and left the area. As soon as he was certain there was no danger present, the jaguar stretched, and then moved to his kill for another meal before abandoning it. He would return to his lair in a more remote area of the ranch and wait for dark to hunt again. Overhead, as high up in the old oak as he could get, the lost monkey hurled insults at the cat along with some pieces of dead wood that he had broken off, all of which were ignored by the jaguar as he finished his meal and moved away from the pond. The remains of the carcass he left to the coyotes and buzzards that had been waiting for their opportunity to feed.

"Well, are you ready to start working?" Otis questioned Tuck as they arrived back at the ranch house.

"I've got my snake boots on and my favorite rifle is in the car with my pack. I believe that I am as ready as I can be," Tuck responded.

"What rifle did you bring, Tuck? I'm a fancier of good guns and own several myself. My personal favorite is a Weatherby Mark five in the .30-378 caliber," Otis was curious about Tuck's rifle.

Tuck went to the car, pulled his drag bag containing the rifle, and laid it up on the hood while he unzipped it. Inside of the case was Tuck's prized Remington 700 with the E.R Shaw fluted barrel chambered for the .308 Winchester round and topped with a Leupold Mark 4 scope. The McMillan stock had been expertly paint camouflaged as had the scope and bolt.

"Whew, all you need now is a ghillie suit and you'd look like a marine sniper!" Otis exclaimed as he admired the tool that his new warden had brought to work.

"It's in the car, Otis, but I hope that I don't need to wear it for this job," Tuck replied with a grin, "Besides most animals can't see you if you sit really still, and from the range that I can hit them with this rifle, they won't see me at all."

Otis liked the young man's confidence, and he realized that there was probably quite a bit that he didn't know about Michael Tucker.

"Tell me about the monkey that is supposed to be out here, Otis. I'm finding that story hard to believe," Tuck asked with a grin.

"Well, I've never seen the monkey, but I've heard him, or something that sounds like some of those National Geographic monkeys. The Mexicans abandoned all of their livestock and pets when they returned to Mexico. There's the white wolf over there, and the peacocks. There were a couple of chickens, and I've seen a big wolf with odd markings on the range. One of their old hands told me about the monkey as he was leaving a couple of weeks ago, and I've been looking for him ever since," Otis replied, "The last place that I heard him was at the waterhole that we checked this morning."

"Well, I'll sure keep an eye out for him. I'd like to start my survey of the wildlife today. Which one of the ATVs do you want me to use?" Tuck asked.

"Take the other one in the shed. It's got a full tank of gas. I'm going to Midland to pick up the truck so hang around until I get back. Julia is fixing some lunch, when you get loaded meet me in the house."

"If it's all the same to you, I packed a light lunch, and I would really like to get started; my apologies to Julia," Tuck replied.

"That's fine, you go on, and I will see you the afternoon…late," Otis said as he walked into the house.

Tuck loaded all of his gear in the back of the ATV and soon was back at the last pond that they had visited that morning, since it was the closest to the house. As he stopped the ATV, a few buzzards flew up and landed in a tree directly above where they had been feeding in the brush. Tuck pulled the Remington 700 from the back, checked that there was a 168-grain Hornady in the chamber, and then eased around the pond and into the brush, very carefully looking for any sign of a predator as he went. The smell from the carcass of the recently killed buck was faint, but it was enough to alert Tuck to the location, and he cautiously moved to where the jaguar had dragged it. After making certain that he was alone except for the buzzards overhead, Tuck knelt to examine the kill. It was immediately obvious to Tuck that the buck had been taken by a large cat, and his neck had been broken. There were deep claw marks in his nose and the puncture marks of four big teeth in the base of his neck well back from his antlers. Predators had eaten almost half of the buck from the shoulders back, and the tracks of the birds and at least two coyotes obliterated any sign of the cat.

After taking a picture with his I-Phone, Tuck removed his K-Bar U.S. Marine Corp fighting knife from its sheath and took the head from the carcass to show to Otis. As he was returning to the ATV, he heard something that sounded odd in the old battered oak tree that stood close to the pond and the area of the kill. Looking up, he saw a small monkey that immediately hid behind the limb that he was clinging to about thirty feet off the ground.

Tuck smiled to himself as he deposited the head in the rack on the ATV, and then cleaned the blood off of his hands in the pond. Returning to his pack, Tuck took an orange that he had packed with his lunch and walked back to the tree to place it in the crotch of the first limb about six feet off of the ground. He didn't know what monkeys ate, but the orange might be a treat for the little primate, and Tuck was determined to befriend it.

As he was returning to he ATV, he heard the sound of the monkey climbing down the oak, and just smiled without turning back to look. Instead, Tuck glanced at the edge of the pond as he walked by and saw the large impressions of the front feet of the jaguar that had been made as the big animal stopped to drink in the late evening after his kill. He quickly took some close up pictures with the I-Phone, and hurried back to the ATV where he had left the rifle. He had several ponds to check before late afternoon, and right now, Tuck wanted to get out to an area more open than where he was standing.

As the afternoon wore on, the weather started to take a change with a few high clouds rolling in, and the temperature dropping. The forecast called for rain in the evening hours, and the extra moisture would be welcomed by every creature that lived here, including Tuck. He missed the climate of the lowlands of South Carolina where he had grown up, but he had also experienced enough deserts during his tours of duty that West Texas seemed like an oasis in comparison. Tuck stopped the ATV on the dirt road just before coming out into a large open area that was ringed with high bluffs and large boulders on the slopes that had fallen from the cliff faces over the years. He picked up his Leupold binoculars and scanned the area of the high ground slowly, looking for any sign of a herd of goats that were supposed to be living there. What he saw on one of the boulders at about four hundred yards startled him. There in all its glory was a very large male cougar, sleeping in the fading sunshine with one paw hanging over the front edge of the big rock. Tuck slowly exited the ATV and got his Remington out of the seat behind him. Quietly pulling the bolt, Tuck checked his zero by bore sighting on the cougar. Then he slowly eased a round into the chamber and set up over the back of the seat for a rest. He laid the crosshairs just on top of the cougar's shoulder as it lay sideways to him, squeezed the trigger, and felt the satisfying thump on his shoulder as the Remington barked.

The cougar jumped straight up in the air at least five feet before flipping off of the boulder face and rolling several yards down the steep slope. Tuck watched through the scope with another round in the chamber as the big cat's tail slowed it twitching and finally was still. Once he was satisfied that the cat was dead, Tuck put the safety on the rifle and drove to within fifty yards of where the cougar lay. Having experienced an up close and personal encounter with these animals on two occasions, he wasn't going to take any chances that thing was playing possum, and so positioned himself to make a slow, careful stalk to his quarry.

The cougar was quite dead when Tuck finally got close enough to him to touch its eyeball with the tip of his gun barrel. As he examined his prize, he was amazed at the size of the big animal's feet. The pads were fully six inches wide, hinting at the two-hundred plus pounds that the cat had attained by killing and eating a deer every week to every week and a half for most of his adult life. Not counted into that number were the 'sport' kills that the cougar would have made periodically, as was the documented habit of the large felines.

Pleased with himself, Tuck moved the ATV close to the dead cat so that he could load it on the back, a task better suited for two men. Once it was secured, Tuck returned to the ranch house to find the young men that helped Otis with the upkeep of the property in hopes that they might skin the cougar for him. Just as he came into view of the bullring, Tuck's cell phone rang with a number that he didn't recognize.

"Hello," He answered

"Tuck this is Julia Jamieson. I thought that you should know that the chief of game wardens for this area is here to meet you," Julia said.

"Thanks Julia, tell him that I am on the way back and will be there shortly"

Tuck drove behind the bullring and rolled the heavy cougar off the back of the ATV. He didn't have his Texas driver's license yet, much less, his hunting license and he wanted to avoid an embarrassing situation.

Tuck drove around the ring to the front of the house where he found the chief of wardens waiting. At six-feet four inches tall and two hundred and fifty pounds, Bob Ledbetter was an impressive individual. He greeted Tuck with a hand outstretched that was as big as a ham.

"Hello Mr. Tucker. I'm Chief of Game Wardens, Robert Ledbetter."

"Hello Warden Ledbetter, I'm Michael Tucker, although everybody calls me Tuck," Tuck replied.

What's that on the back of the ATV?" Ledbetter asked as he walked over to the vehicle to examine the buck's head that Tuck was carrying.

"I found it at one of the water holes. It looks like a big cat may have killed it last night. We think that there is a jaguar running around this ranch, and I thought this might be some of that handiwork. It didn't look like a cougar kill," Tuck replied.

"Have you got a Texas hunting license, Tuck?" Ledbetter asked as he looked over Tuck's Remington."

"No Sir, I'm just getting settled here, and intend to take care of it this next week," Tuck replied.

How many times had he asked the same questions to hunters that were coming through his checkpoint? It certainly felt awkward to be on the receiving end for a change.

"Well, you are going to need that if you are going to be taking heads or killing cats here. I'd like to take this with me if you don't mind. Some of our fellows would like to look at the claw marks on the nose. Where there any other wounds that you could make out?" the Chief Warden asked.

"There was a place at the base of the neck where it looked like a big paper punch had closed over the top of the neck and pierced it in four places.' Tuck replied.

"That's interesting Tuck. What makes you think that a jaguar is out here?"

Well sir, we found a calf the other day that had its head crushed and four tooth holes in the skull. That's not the way a cougar kills, at least none of the ones I've come up against," Tuck answered the question.

"I remember hearing about the troubles that you had in South Carolina with those cats…some other predators too, if I recall. Here's my card. Call me when you get all of your information on this deer herd. I'll be glad to help," Bob Ledbetter turned to leave and then hesitated, "Oh, Tuck, you can bring that cougar around from the bullring now, just make sure to get that license next week."

"Thanks sir, I'll make sure that I have it," Tuck responded lamely. He was embarrassed to have gotten caught with the cat, and for trying to hide it in the first place. His father had taught him better than that. Tuck thought of his dad, and then thought of Harry Albright. It was almost as if his late father-in-law as watching him and shaking his head saying, "Obey the laws of God and man, Tuck."

After Chief of Game Wardens Bob Ledbetter got into his truck and drove away, Tuck got the attention of one of the young men that helped Otis around the ranch, "Hey Antonio, how would you like to make some extra money skinning a cougar for me?" Tuck asked him.

"How big is the cougar, Senor Tuck?" Antonio replied.

"I think about two hundred pounds, give or take. What do you think?" Tuck answered.

"That is a very big cat senor. I will do it for the meat if you don't mind," Antonio looked at Tuck hopefully.

Tuck had never heard of anyone but John Post talk about eating cougars, and he thought it was a joke until now.

"Of course you can have the meat, Antonio, but make sure to skin the head and claws out also, and we have a deal. The cat is behind the bullring," Tuck replied. He wanted the skin for Hanna and Emily, and was glad that Antonio would do the job in trade for the meat.

CHAPTER 8

"What do you mean when you say that you can't find him?" Special Agent Anthony Morris was a little agitated by the report his best field operative was turning in.

"Just that sir, we've used infrared detection methods, ground imaging radar, and good old sift by hand techniques to no avail. Douglas Kensey is gone. It is almost like he left that car and vanished," Joel Biggs stated.

"If only we were that lucky Biggs. That lunatic is a big problem for us, and I would like to get him behind bars. Did Michael Tucker have any reaction to the fact that Kensey was close to where he was staying?" Anthony Morris asked.

"Well, you know how he is. We could have been eating the guy, and Tuck would not have shown any emotion. He only seems to react when there is a threat to his family, so I'm assuming that he did not perceive Kensey's presence to be a threat," Joel Biggs answered.

Anthony Morris was silent for a few seconds, mulling over the information that Joel Biggs had just delivered to him…then, "I believe that Michael Tucker has already had an encounter with the elusive Douglas Kensey, and the outcome wasn't in Kensey's favor. Let's file this under missing and presumed dead. It won't take much to persuade the powers that be that Kensey wandered out on that ranch and got lost. After all, it is a very big place, and there are things out there that could eat him…theoretically speaking of course"

"I understand sir. We'll dismantle the operation here. Do I return to Myrtle Beach?" Biggs was pleased that Tuck was off the hook.

"Only for a short time, you are being transferred to El Paso. They apparently need someone with your special skill set to help with some suspected terrorist cell that is operating out of Juarez," Morris told him.

Joel laughed at the mention of his talents, "Well things were getting boring since Tuck left that area anyway. The change of scenery will do me good."

"I understand perfectly Biggs. Get back as soon as you wrap up there. Director Claiborne wants to debrief you personally," Morris stated before ending the call.

Joel made the calls to end the hunt for Douglas Kensey and returned to his hotel room to finish the reports. There was a certain spring in his step and a smile on his face as he thought of the possibilities that might come his way for a little more adventure, and of course, Michael Tucker would have to know about the transfer.

Special Agent in Charge, Noah Escobar, sat in his El Paso office fuming at the report that had just come in regarding the wreckage of a light plane that had been found by a rancher in a remote area of Texas, south of Sheffield. The plane's fuselage numbers corresponded with one that agents had tried to stop two weeks before in Chihuahua before it could take off with four suspected Islamic terrorists on board. To make matters worse, there was only the body of the pilot found in the wreckage, meaning that now there was an Islamic terror cell loose somewhere on U.S. soil and this had happened on Noah's watch.

"Idiots!" he exclaimed in anger as he slammed his fist into the desktop with a loud bang.

"Sir, are you alright?" came the voice of his secretary, Lois Freeman from the front office.

"Yes, yes, just get me Director Claiborne on a secure line will you Lois?" Noah answered as he hugged his bruised fist close to his body in an effort to stop the pain.

Several minutes passed before the phone on his desk rang. Noah Escobar knew that the news he was going to give to the Deputy Director of the FBI would not bring a favorable response from this powerful man, but he was a man of duty, and this news needed to be sent up the chain of command.

"This is Special Agent Escobar speaking," Noah answered the phone.

"Hello Escobar, what is the urgent message that your secretary called me about?" Director Claiborne asked.

"Sir, I need to report that an action to stop a plane loaded with four suspected Islamic terrorists failed, and these men are somewhere in the United States as we speak," Noah replied.

"I don't remember receiving any report of an impending action taking place in Mexico, Escobar. Who exactly authorized this strike?" Claiborne asked.

Noah's mouth felt like it was full of cotton, and he was certain that his retirement fund was going to be shortened significantly when he answered, "Two weeks ago I reported the need for a strategic action against this group down in Chihuahua to the DHS head for this area. He authorized us to stop the plane with non-lethal force before it could take off. We did not succeed, and the plane managed to fly across the border during a diversion at the crossing."

"Escobar, I am going to tell you something that might save your pension so listen carefully. There are no, and I repeat no Islamic terrorists operating on United States soil! Do you understand?"

"Yes sir, at least I think that I do. Can you clarify that for me?" Noah Escobar answered.

"The president does not want to stir up the American people against the Muslims that live here, so we are to not to refer to any Islamic fighters crossing our border as terrorists.

They are now to be referred to as 'Freedom Fighters'. Am I clear?" Director Claiborne asked.

"Perfectly clear sir," Noah answered in disgust. Thank God, he only had to make it through the next two years to secure his pension. He had a feeling that it would be the longest two years of his life.

"Very well, send me a report on the plane. From now on everything that we do out there regarding 'Freedom Fighters' gets reported directly to me, and to me alone. I've also arranged to have a special operator transferred to El Paso from the Myrtle Beach office. I thought that I was being pre-emptive on this, but it looks like the action may be a little late. In any regard, his group will be the ones handling any covert ops from your office," Director Claiborne finished the call and hung up leaving Noah Escobar with more questions than answers.

"Lois, will you get me an appointment set up to have my blood pressure checked? While you're at it, please call my wife and tell her that I'll be late getting home tonight...paper work, case loads, etc," Noah called into his secretary.

"Yes sir, I'll get right on it. By the way, do you want to make reservations for us tonight? I know a great little place close to the border where no one will run into us," Lois replied sweetly.

"That sounds great! I'll wrap things up here so we can get an early start. You sure know how to pick up an old man's spirits," Noah sounded excited as he anticipated his illicit rendezvous with his secretary. After all, who would ever know?

Little did he know how much the old proverb that things done in the dark would be revealed in the light would affect him and so many others after tonight. As soon as Lois made reservations, she sent a simple text, "Everything is a go."

CHAPTER 9

Tuck had just finished tacking the skin of the big cougar to the shaded side of one of the sheds near the ranch house and rubbing in a coating of salt to preserve it, when Otis returned with a lightly used, late model Ford F-250 crew cab, four-wheel drive truck. Tuck walked over with a grin on his face that gave away his excitement at not having to drive the Buick anymore.

"That is a lot more truck than I expected, Otis," Tuck said as he walked around the big vehicle.

"Well, out here a lot depends an whether your equipment is up to the task or not, and I figured this one would get just about any job done that you would need to do on the ranch," Otis replied.

"I imagine it will at that," Tuck said, "By the way, I shot a big cougar while you were gone. Caught him taking a nap on a big rock west of here about a mile and pretty close to where the goats are supposed to be. There was also a dead buck at that waterhole where we stopped this morning. I think our jaguar friend was in there while we walked around. I brought the head back, but Warden Ledbetter took it for examination. He wasn't too pleased with me killing that cougar without a license, but cut me a mile of slack though. Oh, and I saw the monkey," Tuck finished his report.

"Man, you've had a busy first day, haven't you?" Otis asked rhetorically, "Let's go inside and I'll get your check. I know you're probably anxious to get back to Hanna and the baby. Do you think she can stand the ride down her? We'd like to see her before taking off next week if she's up to it. By the way, park the Buick over by the other vehicles before you leave. You can pick it up when it suits you, and it will be out of the way over there"

"Thanks Otis. I'll check with her when I get back. If I know Hanna, she's ready to get out of the house," Tuck replied.

"Well, don't rush her Tuck," Julia had come out to where the men were talking, "It takes some time to heal up from childbirth, both physically and emotionally. Men don't have any understanding about that…or a lot of other things where we women are concerned," She gave Otis a big smile and a kiss on the cheek when she had finished and handed him Tuck's check. He just rolled his eyes.

"Yes ma'am, I'm sure we don't…at least I don't, but I'm learning," Tuck said with a laugh, "I'd better get that car put up and head back home. Hanna will be worried about me. I'll see you all in the morning."

Six bump gates and a few miles of dirt road later Tuck was back on the road and headed for Odessa. He needed to call Luke and find out what he knew about jaguar hunting or if he knew of somebody that did.

"Hey Tuck, what's going on?" Luke answered his phone.

"Hi Luke, do you know anything about hunting jaguars?" Tuck asked.

"I know that they can be mean suckers. We used to see them from time to time when I was growing up, but there aren't many around anymore. Did you find that one on Otis' ranch?" Luke replied.

"Not exactly, but I found his breakfast. I do need to get this jaguar off of the ranch though, any thoughts about how we are going to do it?" Tuck asked, hoping that Luke might know of somebody that could help.

"Well, there is a state trapper that comes to all of the gun shows. From what I've heard, there isn't much in the way of predators that he hasn't trapped. Let me call around and see if I can't get a contact number for him. Call me when you get back in Odessa," Luke replied.

"Thanks Luke. I hope you'll be able to hunt with us when we get everything set up."

"I wouldn't want to miss that one, Tuck," Luke said as he ended the call.

Tuck was just getting ready to call Hanna when his phone rang, "Hey Tuck, it's Joel. I just wanted to give you a call and tell you that the FBI has ended the search for Doug Kensey and will mark him off as 'missing and presumed dead."

"That's good news, I suppose. Are you headed back East then Joel?" Tuck asked.

"That's the second part of my news, Tuck. I'm being transferred to El Paso as soon as the director debriefs me," Joel answered.

"That sounds good, Joel," Tuck replied, although he wasn't certain if it was good or not.

"I'll call when I get settled out there. Maybe we can do some hunting together," Joel suggested.

"Well, it certainly looks like there will be a lot of that just to clean this ranch up, Joel. Maybe we can. Have a good trip back and tell Agent Morris hello for me," Tuck said, hoping the call was finished. There was something about talking to the Feds that irritated him, although Joel had certainly seemed like one of the good guys.

"I will, Tuck. You have my cell number. Give me a call if anything comes up before I get back," Joel ended the call.

Tuck mulled over Joel's news for a few minutes before calling Hanna to tell her about the day. They talked for the next half-an-hour until the phone battery was almost dead before Tuck ended the call with a laugh. Tuck really enjoyed the company of his wife, and he was determined to get her to the ranch as soon as possible, so they could share the beauty of the place together, and so he could protect his family.

CHAPTER 10

Maria Hernandez answered her husband's phone to keep from waking him from the nap that he had taken after coming in from work early in the day, "Hello, Manny's phone."

"Yes ma'am, this is Michael Tucker. Is Manny available?" Tuck asked.

"Senor Tucker, Manny told me about the panther down on the Thunder Ranch. He was so upset that I insisted he lay down for a little while. Can he call you back a little later?" She asked in a hushed voice.

"Certainly, Mrs. Hernandez; please tell Manny that we are going to arrange a hunt for the jaguar and that he is invited, as I promised," Tuck replied.

"I am very worried about my husband, Senor Tucker. This hunt might be the only thing that will bring closure to the dreams that haunt his sleep," Maria told Tuck.

"Well, you know that this is cannot be the same animal that Manny saw thirty years ago. I mean, jaguars don't live that long," Tuck replied.

"I know, but he is under some kind of attack from this devil cat every time he closes his eyes. Until he sees it is dead, there will be no peace for him," Maria sounded worried for her husband.

Harry Albright had taught Tuck well in the short time that he was both Tuck's pastor and father-in-law. One of the things that he said often was that a curse without cause would not light, and that it took one in a higher position than the person creating the curse to lift it. Tuck didn't tell Maria any of this, but he knew that killing the cat would not free Manny from what he had locked in his mind. Only one thing would, and Tuck was determined to share that knowledge with Manny as soon as possible.

"I understand, Mrs. Hernandez. Tell Manny that I'll call him as soon as we have a firm time for the hunt," Tuck gave his regards and ended the call.

"Tuck, dinner's almost ready," Kathryn's voice called from the kitchen of the bunkhouse.

"Yes ma'am. I've got one more short call to make and then I'll be in," Tuck called back.

He dialed Luke's number hoping to have an answer to the problem of hunting the panther.

"Tuck, I've got good news! I found the trapper that I was telling you about, and he can meet us down there tomorrow to look the place over. If there is a panther there, he will arrange to have a fellow from Arizona bring his dogs up so we can run it to tree. What do you think?" Luke gave Tuck the news.

"I think that we need to meet for breakfast. You can ride down with me in the new truck that Otis is providing. Pack a lunch because it will probably be a long day," Tuck answered, "Oh, and Luke, you probably should have a piece with you, just in case."

"That sounds good to me, Tuck. I'll see you at the Wagon Wheel at six o'clock sharp," Luke finished the call.

Tuck walked into the kitchen and gave his stepmother-in-law a hug, "Kathryn, I sure am glad that you are here with Hanna and Emily."

"I wouldn't want to be anywhere else, Michael. Besides, the way that you eat, Hanna needs help in the kitchen," She teased.

"I heard my name mentioned," Hanna called from the bedroom where she was nursing Emily.

"Just saying good things, Hon," Tuck responded with a laugh, "Otis and Julia want you to come to the ranch before they leave for the Alaskan trip next week. Do you feel up to the trip?

Hanna came into the kitchen as she replied with a smile, "Shhh, you'll wake the baby. I think that I might be able to ride down by the weekend. What do you think, Mom?"

At the word 'Mom', Kathryn's eyes teared up, "I think that as long as I can go too, it would be wonderful, and she gave Hanna a hug, "Now let's eat before it gets cold."

The rest of the evening was spent with Tuck regaling them with his story of the day that he had at the ranch, and Hanna sharing her day with him. Tuck held Emily on his chest after she woke up, and thought of little else besides how good she smelled with her little head pressed under his chin.

Tuck and Luke arrived at the ranch at eight o'clock to find the state trapper, a wiry man about five feet nine inches tall and one hundred and sixty pounds, waiting for them with Otis outside of the ranch house. Otis made the introductions.

"Tuck, Luke, this is Avery Newsome, the state trapper that you called. He's ready to look around for this jaguar, if it's here."

"Well, we're ready to go as soon as I get our gear out of the truck, Mr. Newsome," Tuck replied as he shook Avery's calloused hand.

"I talked to Warden Ledbetter on the way over this morning. His people believe that this might be a jaguar also, and they want it taken alive, if possible. Once we can find an area where it's been hunting, I'll make the call for some dogs, and we'll try to get him in close enough to dart him with a tranquilizer gun. The first place that I'd like to look would be where you found the buck's carcass," Avery explained the plan to them.

"Tuck, I've got the ATVs both fueled so take your pick. I'd like to tag along too. I've never seen one of these cats, and this promises to be kind of exciting," Otis said to Tuck.

"Sure thing Otis, I was hoping that you'd come along since you know this place better than anyone around," Tuck responded, "I'll grab our stuff out of the truck."

Once they were ready to head out, Luke reached into his backpack and pulled out a 1911 Rock Island .45ACP and slid the holster onto his belt. Tuck stuck his rifle in the rack overhead, and Otis checked his Mossberg 500 tactical before loading it in the overhead also. Avery Newsome had an older Ruger Bearcat .22 slung in a shoulder rig that was his trademark.

The trip to the waterhole where Tuck had found the buck took about twenty minutes. They got out of the ATV and walked to the edge of the pond where the tracks of the jaguar were still visible.

"That is a big cat, Tuck. I'm guessing around two-fifty or more," Avery told them after studying the size of the foot and the depth of the track, "These animals are not like the cougar, and can be very dangerous, which is why they were hunted out of this range a long time ago. If we run into it, do not make eye contact."

He stood up and looked around the waterhole carefully for any other sign before moving in the direction that Tuck indicated where they would find what was left of the carcass.

As they walked around the water hole, Tuck took a banana out of his pack and placed it in the high fork of the oak when they walked by.

"What's that for?" Luke asked.

"You'll see when we get back, if it's still here," Tuck answered without any other explanation, then pointing, "I found the buck back there."

Avery eased to the spot where the remains of the deer were now scattered, and checked the ground for any sign of the jaguar's presence.

"Nothing here," He announced after about five minutes, "the cat probably saw you in here and went back to its lair."

"How do we find that?" Otis asked.

"Well, they seem to like dense vegetation and water. Unlike most cats, these things are strong swimmers, so I'm thinking that we check around the other waterholes for sign," Avery answered.

"If that is the case, then we need to head to the high tank first. The area around that tank is heavily covered in growth, offers a good view of the area, and is very close to some of the caves that are in the cliff faces around here," Otis said.

"Sounds like a plan to me," Tuck added as they walked back around the oak where the banana was placed.

"Tuck, the banana is gone!" Luke exclaimed as they walked by.

Tuck looked up into the top of the tree to see the monkey sitting in full view, peeling the banana, "There's your mystery monkey, Otis."

The men stood for a minute just watching the little animal that seemed oblivious to their presence.

"Tuck, I'll keep the fruit for this little guy at the house for you to feed him everyday. Let's see if you can't get him to follow you home in a week or two. We'll have some colder weather coming in, and I'd really like to get him somewhere warm for the winter," Otis said.

"I was thinking the same thing, Otis. It would be a shame for the monkey to survive being abandoned only to freeze to death," Tuck replied, then, "How about you driving. I can't remember how to get to the high tank."

The men raced off to the high ground with Otis driving the ATV like a sports car on the narrow trail. As they started the climb to the tank, Avery tapped Otis on the shoulder and signaled him to stop.

"Look down there about a hundred yards. Isn't that a cow down on her side?" He asked pointing downhill at a black mound among the mesquite.

Otis picked up his binoculars from the dash of the ATV and looked, "It's not moving, let's get down there, and have a look."

Tuck reached for his rifle as he got out of the ATV, and the others followed suit. Luke racked the slide on the 1911 and slid the safety upward to lock the hammer before putting it back in his holster 'cocked and locked', an action that did not go unnoticed by the other men.

He saw them looking at him and said, "I saw how fast these things are when I was a kid. If we jump this one and it turns on us, you men won't have time to rack a round into your firearms before it gets to you."

"He's right," Avery backed Luke up, "I don't think we'll come up on it, but it doesn't hurt to be safe."

As Avery finished, Tuck stroked the bolt on the .308 and slid the safety on, and Otis worked the slide on the shotgun before they carefully made their way through the brush to where the cow lay.

All of a sudden, Luke shouted, "Holy Crap!" and jumped back a full three feet while digging for his .45. The loud blast of Otis's shotgun ripped the air before the .45 could clear leather.

Writhing on the ground directly in front of Luke was a headless six-foot diamond back rattlesnake that was as big around as his wrist.

"Good shootin', Otis!" Luke declared, "As soon as I get my britches cleaned out, we can go see the cow."

The other three men were laughing at the way Luke had reacted to the snake.

"You move pretty fast for an old guy," Tuck told him jokingly.

"I got bitten by one about that size when I was a young man. They scare the crap out of me even when I can see them, much less almost step on one," Luke replied.

Otis stooped down to cut the rattles off and put them in his pocket, "Unless somebody wants to eat him, I'm just going to leave it there."

"You Texans have some really strange dietary habits," Tuck told him as he walked past the snake to where the cow was lying, "She's deader than a doornail, and her head has been crushed like the other one!"

Avery and Otis stooped to examine the cow that had been freshly killed only a few hours before. The head showed the evidence of the jaguar's powerful bite marks, and the hindquarters had been torn into with the blood still dripping fresh and warm from the torn flesh.

"We ran that cat off of the kill, and I'll bet a dollar to a donut that it's close by just watching us so let's just back out real easy. I'm going to call for the dogs as soon as we get clear of the area," Avery told them.

Luke slid the 1911 out of his holster and held it in his hand as they moved slowly back to the ATV, not taking their eyes off of the cow until they were a hundred yards away from the kill area. Otis drove them back to the ranch while Avery made the call to his contact in Arizona.

Avery argued with the dog handler who didn't want to make the drive until the next day, "I know it's a long hump up here, but if you leave now, you can get your dogs on a fresh trail in the morning. They are calling for rain late tomorrow evening, and the dogs won't have the scent trail that will still be fresh in the morning is all I'm saying. Yes, Texas will pay your expenses. I'm authorized to sign your invoice so let's get this thing rolling. Okay, we'll see you late this evening."

Avery finished the call and then turned to the others, "Well, he is going to leave Rodeo, New Mexico in a couple of hours, so we are going to have a hunt in the morning. I'd like to start at first light where we found the cow. Warden Ledbetter wants two of his men here to handle the dart guns, and to make sure we don't kill the cat unless it is absolutely necessary."

Tuck was reminded of how the dog hunt turned out for the South Carolina cougar, and hoped this one would be more productive. He wished that Bob Pike were here with him. They had made a good team, and had shared quite a few exciting moments. He made up his mind to call Bob when this hunt was over.

"Well, if we are going to start this hunt at 'O Dark Thirty', then I am going home and get prepared for it," Tuck said to Otis, "We need to get hold of Manny Hernandez too. He told us to let him know when the hunt was scheduled so he could go along for 'therapy' or something like that."

"Actually, the more of us that there are, the less chance we have of that cat running back through us if the dogs get him cornered up there somewhere," Avery mentioned.

"Okay then, Tuck. We'll see you back here at about five o'clock in the morning then. We'll want those dogs up there at first light."

Luke and Tuck loaded the truck and started the long drive back to Goldsmith. Tuck called Manny and left word with Maria for him to be at the Thunder Ranch at five am if he wanted to help catch that jaguar, and then he called Hanna to let her know that he was headed in early.

"I think that's great Michael. Kathryn wanted to keep Emily so we can go out for dinner before she left, and this would be a great time," Hanna told him.

"As long as I can get to bed early, I'll do anything you want, love," Michael agreed. It would be good to spend a little private time with Hanna tonight.

After ending the call, Tuck said to Luke, "Well, what did you think?"

"I think you should pull into that Stripes in McCamey, and let me get some coffee and a bite to eat. Getting the crap scared out of me twice in one day makes me hungry," Luke answered with a grin.

"I could use a little coffee myself. It did get interesting for a little bit, didn't it? I was thinking of how fast those big cats can move when they want to, and in that cover there wouldn't have been much time to get a shot off," Tuck replied.

"That's exactly what I was thinking, plus that I was getting too old for that kind of excitement, but after we got back to the ranch house, I realized that I kind of enjoyed it," Luke laughed at the thought.

"I'm going by the gun shop on the way home and see if he has a decent riot gun on the rack. I definitely am carrying a shotgun tomorrow in case those drugs don't work fast enough!" Tuck told him.

"That sounds good, just don't miss the Stripes up there," Luke reminded him, "My stomach is growling like one of those cats.

Earlier, the panther had watched the men approach his kill with every muscle ready to attack. A low growl started in his throat, and he started a slow and deliberate stalk to attack the intruders when the sound of the shotgun made him freeze in place. No stranger to being shot at, he stayed hidden in the dark shadow of a big mesquite bush until the men were gone. The jaguar then returned warily to his meal, tearing the flesh of the hindquarters in large chunks, and pulverizing the bone with its powerful jaws that were capable of crushing the skulls of most mammals and driving the teeth into their brains.

The black jaguar fed for most of an hour, then returned to the mesquite to rest before feeding again. Unlike the cougar, the jaguar didn't cover or try to hide his prey. He would drive off any interlopers until he was finished with it, and then abandon the carcass to the coyotes and buzzards.

Late that evening, the big cat moved to his rock lair just above the big water tank on the high ground.

CHAPTER 11

As planned, the men assembled at the ranch house at five the next morning. Julia had coffee made and enough eggs, bacon, and potatoes fixed to feed a small army. Introductions were made all around, and Avery introduced Tyler Whitehall as the houndsman that would be leading the hunt with his three dogs, one blue tick, and two redbone hounds. The game wardens showed up at six with the dart guns. Otis gave them their own ATV, and he, Manny, Tuck and Luke took the other one and led the wardens, and the truck with the dogs to the spot where the jaguar had made his last kill.

Tyler had telemetry collars on all of the dogs, and led them down to the carcass of the cow, or what was left of it after the coyotes had finished.

The dogs were casting about for several minutes before the blue tick, Dallas, came across the mesquite where the big jaguar had napped. He broke out in a loud voice and started casting around, looking for the trail that the cat had left. Soon he was joined by Lafayette, and Claude, the two redbones, and the pack took off for the high ground in full voice.

Tyler stood looking proudly after his dogs and said, "Fellas, I think we have a cat. We'll go back to the ATV and let them work for a bit, and then I'll track them to the cat."

"Tyler, have your dogs run a jaguar before?" Tuck asked him on the way back to the ATV.

"I've had them treed twice, but they broke through the pack and escaped. They are a quite a bit more aggressive than a cougar, and they will attack the dog handler sometimes. Avery can tell you about that. Just don't make eye contact with this one if we get him cornered in those rocks," He admonished.

Tuck could tell that Manny was nervous about this business, and Luke was carrying the 1911 'cocked and locked'. He had left the used Remington 870 that he'd purchased the night before in the ATV since he didn't have a license, and he was pretty certain that Warden Ledbetter had probably shared that information. While they waited, he decided to strike up a conversation with the two game wardens that were getting their equipment ready.

"How fast will that stuff work on a jaguar if you get to dart him?" Tuck asked.

"Hell, we don't know. We've never done this before. I'm thinking that we will have to shoot him anyway, but those environmentalists will sure be upset if we do," The taller of the two responded, "You're that warden from South Carolina that Chief Ledbetter told us about, aren't you?"

"Yep, I won't ever get away from that mess," Tuck replied to the question.

"Well we followed that story real close out here, and a bunch of us want you to know that you did a hell of a job. Some of the guys were taking bets on whether you were going to make it or not. No offense," The other one said.

"None taken, I wasn't sure we would either," Tuck replied wanting to change the subject, "I'm going to try and improve the deer herd on this ranch for Otis, and I'll probably need your help at some point."

"You've got it when you need it. We had to draw straws to see who would get to work with you on this hunt. Some of the guys from around Alpine even volunteered. Man, you're a hero to a bunch of us including Chief Ledbetter, although he probably won't admit it straight out."

"That means a lot to me, but I just want to stay off of the radar now," Tuck was thoroughly embarrassed by the accolades he was receiving from these men.

"Hey," the shorter one said, "we have been rotating out with the other game wardens in the trans-Pecos region down on the river pulling river patrol duty. I'll bet they would let you come along if I asked Chief Ledbetter. What do you think?"

"It sounds interesting. Maybe when I get settled in here we can get together on it," Tuck responded, hoping that the topic wouldn't come up again. He had it up to his ears with law enforcement, and just wanted to be left alone.

Tuck heard the dogs suddenly start baying continuously, "Something is happening fellows."

Avery came back to the second ATV and told them that the cat was cornered. The two wardens grabbed their dart guns and piled into their ATV. Tyler and Avery had jumped in the truck and headed up the steep trail to where the collar telemetry indicated the dogs were. Otis, Tuck, Luke, and a very nervous Manny Hernandez loaded into the ATV and followed the parade to the water tank at the top of the rise. The tank was a round concrete structure that was about fifteen feet across and six feet high on the low side of slope. It was fed by a solar powered pump that had replaced the rickety windmill that had been the standard equipment in the west for years. The dogs were about three hundred yards past the tank up in the rock-strewn area just below the bluff that had several caves eroded into its surface.

"They've got him in one of the caves!" Otis exclaimed.

"Maybe," Tyler responded, "but be ready for him to be above you when we get up there."

The two wardens led the way with their dart rifles loaded and at the ready. Luke had his 1911 in his hand while Otis and Tuck carried their shotguns. Manny was ashen in color from fear, and wouldn't leave the ATV that was parked closest to the tank.

"Manny, if you don't want to come, yo
Tuck told him as they started to leave the ar
times like this. It will pass."

"I just keep remembering the eyes, Senor Tuck. It had the eyes of a devil," Manny replied.

"Well, keep alert, and keep that shotgun of yours ready…just in case," Tuck answered as he walked off after the others.

Whether he knew it or not, Manny Hernandez was on the verge of a breakdown, and Tuck was questioning the wisdom in bringing him on this hunt.

As they got closer to the cave, they could see the dogs worked up into a lather at the cave entrance. The scent of the cat must be overpowering for them to be that bold, Tuck thought. They were jumping back and forth, and baying non-stop now, a sure signal that their quarry was holed up in front of them.

Tyler led the two wardens in slowly, checking every rock for a sign that the very dangerous animal wasn't above them somehow. They approached the cave entrance that was about three feet high; the dart rifles raised in position, and Tyler had a double-barreled shotgun at the ready as a backup.

As they illuminated the dark cave with a flashlight from behind the dogs, one of the wardens said, "I don't believe the cat is in there. I can see the back of the cave."

Tyler got the leashes on his dogs and pulled them back while the wardens held their position in case the cat ran out of the hole in the rock. Nothing happened; the cat had eluded the dogs!

Suddenly from the direction of the tank, there came a blood-curdling scream followed closely by a shotgun blast, and then another scream, this time much weaker.

"The panther got Manny!" Otis shouted and they all started at a run for the tank, hoping to reach it in time to save Manny's life.

Tuck was the first to reach the tank, and dreaded what he would find when he came around to the ATVs. The first thing that he saw was Manny's body lying on his back next to the ATV. The shotgun was beside him, but there was a huge hole blown in the top of the ATV. There were also the tracks of the cat close to Manny, shoved deep into the damp ground indicating that he had jumped from the tank down on his victim. Tuck knelt beside the body and felt the throat for any sign of life as the others came around the tank.

"Is he dead Tuck?" Otis asked.

Tuck started to laugh, "Manny fainted! I think the cat may have been in that tank when we got here and jumped out which scared Manny spitless. He sure killed the top of the ATV though, and I'll bet that jaguar crapped on himself when Manny started screaming."

The men were laughing so hard that it was a few minutes before Avery thought to splash a little water in Manny's face.

"What happened? Am I dead?" He asked as he sat up.

"It looks like you passed out when the cat came out of the tank," Avery told him with a chuckle, "What exactly happened?"

"I turned to look back over my shoulder and saw that black panther of my dreams coming over the edge of the tank right at me. The next thing that I remember was just now waking up. Oh Hell, I crapped in my pants!" Manny exclaimed, looking down at his britches.

"You shot a hole in the top of my ATV!" Otis exclaimed.

Tyler then said, "That gun going off probably saved his life. What do you want to do now?"

"You came here to run that cat down, turn the dogs loose!" Avery replied.

Tuck walked over and helped Manny to his feet, "Take the shot up ATV back to the ranch house, Manny. You probably want to get home after this. We'll double up when we come back."

"I think I will Senor Tuck, my apologies for the damage, my company will make it right," Manny said as he got in the ATV and left the group at the tank. Otis just stood there shaking his head.

The dogs picked up the cat's scent immediately and took off in full voice after him directly through some of the roughest terrain on the ranch.

"I think that I know where he is going," Otis said, "Let's see if we can't get in front of him."

They piled in the remaining ATV and drove down the hill to a road that ran in the general direction the cat was moving. Otis had the ATV wide open down the dirt trial with Tyler and the two wardens directly behind in his truck, when Tyler blew the horn and signaled him to stop.

"They're not moving," He shouted from the truck window and gestured to the south into a very dense mesquite covered gully, "I think he's gone to tree."

Otis drove slowly over to the gully and shut off the ATV. They could hear the excited baying of the dogs about two hundred yards in.

Avery stood and listened for about two minutes with the rest of them, "What do you think Tyler?'

"I think we need to get in there and tranq that cat before he kills the dogs," Tyler replied.

They made their way down into the brushy bottom where the mesquite was over their heads, making a visual on the dogs difficult. Finally, they were close enough to see movement through the bushes, and the two game wardens moved in closer to the treed animal. The dogs were in full voice at a yellow jaguar that had backed up into a large stand of mesquite with no place to go but over the dogs.

"Shoot it quick guys He's getting ready to charge us!" Avery shouted.

Both dart guns went off almost simultaneously just as the cat ran through the dog pack like hot knife through butter, accompanied by the high-pitched yelp of an injured dog. With the exception of Tuck, all of the men scattered away from the cat as it lunged. Tuck stood his ground with the Remington 870 held in front of him, pointed at the jaguar that suddenly folded up and slid right up to his feet.

The other wardens came back to where the cat was lying with expressions of shock on their faces.

"Man you are one cool character, Tuck!" the shorter of the two exclaimed, "How did you know that it wasn't going to run over you?"

"I didn't, but I couldn't shoot it without my license," Tuck replied in jest as he knelt beside the drugged jaguar, "Didn't Manny tell us that the cat of his dreams came out of that tank?"

"That's not the right cat, Tuck! Manny's cat is black!" Luke exclaimed.

"That's exactly right! Gentlemen, we have at least two of these cats in here, and this one is a big female. What's the next plan of action?" Tuck asked.

"We have to get this one immobilized and transported before the drugs wear off, so there is nothing more we can do about the other one tonight," The taller of the game wardens responded.

Tyler then said, "I've got to get these dogs back, and tended to. Old Claude got scratched up a bit. I don't know when I can get back. We're booked for cougar hunts for at least the next three weeks."

"Well, I guess that answers that question, but the day has not been a loss. The State of Texas has a live jaguar in its collection. We've got one less killing our stock, and Manny met up with his nightmare. This has been a good day," Tuck told the group.

"Tuck's right, let's call it a day and get back to the ranch house. I've had enough excitement to do me for two years," Otis said with a smile.

The wardens tied the sleeping cat with cord that was carried for the purpose, and then went to the truck for the stretcher they had put in the back. Soon the animal was loaded on top of the dog box, Tyler loaded his hounds, and the whole group made the way slowly to the ranch house.

Once the dogs had quieted, the Black Panther circled back to his lair in the rocks above the water tank and rested. This wasn't the first time that he had been hunted, and he had no fear of the two-legged animal that had occasionally been a food source for him. When evening came, he would kill again.

CHAPTER 12

Lois' brown eyes held a smiling promise as she handed Noah his second margarita of the night at the Hacienda Montana Cantina in old Juarez. She let her hand stay for just the moment longer than was necessary to hand him his drink, and Noah's pulse quickened as their fingers touched. Like a spider weaving her web for a juicy fly, Lois plied her tradecraft with exquisite charm.

As Noah finished his drink, the sedative took control and he slumped slightly in his chair as the room spun and grew dark. The two businessmen at an adjoining table quickly helped Lois get him to his feet and then whisked him to a waiting car in the restaurant parking lot as Lois paid the tab with a large cash tip for the waiter, his reward for silence. They had left Noah's official vehicle in El Paso in a truck stop parking lot before taking her car across the border, so she now followed the late model Mercedes in her car as it took the unfortunate Special Agent Noah Escobar on a one-way ride into the desolate territory of Chihuahua.

"No sir, she hasn't come in either. Yes sir, the police found his car this morning, and I have men going through it now. We've also gotten the street camera feeds from last night for a six-block radius of where the car was found. They show Agent Escobar getting into the car with his secretary and driving off. Her car crossed into Juarez at nine fifteen last night, and security video there shows Agent Escobar was not under noticeable duress. Yes sir, I will keep you posted on any new developments," Second in command, Agent Walter Grooms wiped the sweat from his head after talking to Director Claiborne in the Washington Bureau about the disappearance of Noah Escobar.

"Listen up folks," he spoke loudly to be heard above the noise of the room, "We will have a team from Washington here late tonight or in the morning. I want to have some of the things that they ask for ready to hand to them when they get here. Get a full background check on Lois Freeman. I don't think that was done when she was hired. Find something with her DNA on it and get that analyzed. In addition, I want a couple of you to get over to Noah's house and talk to his wife before the locals hear about this. She doesn't need to learn about her husband on the morning news! The clock is running, and we need to follow every lead if we are going to find him with all of his body parts intact."

Agent Grooms knew that there was always a possibility that Special Agent Escobar had been kidnapped for ransom, but that was an unlikely scenario given the fact that his secretary was seen rendezvousing with him after he parked his car. She was the key to finding the reason for Escobar's disappearance, but first they would need to find out more about her.

"SIR!" A shout came from a young agent that was walking quickly to where Walter was standing, "I think we may have something on Lois here."

"What do you have Max?" Walter asked.

"Lois Freeman is not Lois Freeman!" He exclaimed, "She is Lois Salinas, the sister of one Pablo Salinas the son of Isaiah Salinas. In case you don't remember that name, Special Agent Escobar and a deep cover operative named Bradley Rumskill undertook a raid on a Los Zetas' stronghold twenty years ago to free a female agent that had been taken hostage. The agent was killed in the attack, as was Isaiah Salinas, the leader of that branch of Los Zetas."

"So Lois was able to infiltrate our office because Noah has always been a skirt chaser, and now all of our data is compromised, including the identity of anyone in the witness protection program here. Great, just great!" Walter sat heavily back into his desk chair and reached for the phone. Director Claiborne needed to know this information immediately.

Deputy Director of the FBI, John Claiborne, sat behind his desk looking at the phone that had brought the news of Special Agent Noah Escobar's disappearance. He and Noah Escobar had been young agents together when they teamed up with Bradley Rumskill to try and rescue their fellow agent and Bradley's partner from the hands of the Los Zetas, a rescue attempt that was anything but successful. Not only had the kidnapped agent died in the attempt, but Bradley, blinded by rage and grief at the loss of his partner, executed six of the disarmed Los Zetas members including Isaiah Salinas, the leader of the group before Noah was able to disarm him. His actions brought a vendetta against him, so the FBI put Bradley into the witness protection program and sealed the records masking the identity of all the agents that had taken part in the raid.

With the security of the El Paso office breached and Noah missing, John Claiborne needed to bring his big guns to bear before the gang made good on another twenty-year-old threat against those responsible for the deaths of Isaiah Salinas and his men. It was time to call in all of the favors owed to him. Little did he know that the clock had started running almost two weeks before when Noah's agents failed to stop the flight into Texas from Mexico.

CHAPTER 13

Hanna, Kathryn, and Emily made the trip with Tuck to the Thunder Ranch to meet Otis and Julia on the day before they left for a month long trip to Alaska. Both women were fascinated with how the Texas landscape changed from a flat and dirty looking desert filled with pump jacks, drilling rigs, pipe yards and hundreds of RVs in man-camps that barely met the minimal requirements in a largely no code environment, to a picturesque western scene with rolling hills, cattle, cactus and mesquite that personified the beauty of a hundred classic cowboy movies. It looked as if at any minute, John Wayne would come over a small rise, riding shotgun on a stagecoach being chased by Indians.

"Well, here we are ladies," Tuck announced as they turned off of the interstate highway feeder and pulled up to the first of several 'bump' gates that controlled the traffic on the ranch road.

"Tuck, you're going to hit that gate!" Hanna exclaimed as Tuck showed no sign of stopping the forward roll of the Ford truck.

"That's the idea, Honey," Tuck told her as he bumped the gate with the cowcatcher mounted on the front of the truck. The gate swung open as they passed through, and then closed behind them.

"The trick is to hit it just hard enough to make it swing out of the way and still give you plenty of time to get through. Otherwise the gate will hit the side of the vehicle," Tuck told her as he laughed at the expression on Hanna's face.

"How many are there, Tuck?" Kathryn asked from the back seat.

"Five more on this road, and quite a few on the rest of the ranch," Tuck answered, "they are necessary to keep the cattle from wondering out of their range. The cows are afraid to cross the open pipes across the road,"

The two women were spellbound by the scenery and the immense size of the country surrounding them and asked question after question until Tuck pulled up at the ranch house where Otis and Julia were waiting. After the introductions were made, Julia took Emily in her arms, and invited Hanna and Kathryn to follow her into the house. Tuck and Otis walked back to the old foreman's trailer where several contractors were busy with a cleanup and renovations.

"Well, what do you think?" Otis asked.

"It looks like it is going to be pretty nice when they finish," Tuck answered although he didn't think much of trailers in general.

"Well, try not to show too much excitement, Tuck. It will be fine when they get all of the work done. I'm having them turn one of the bedrooms into a nursery for little Emily. Before you go back tonight, let me know what color Hanna wants in there, and we'll see to it. I've got a friend picking us up in the morning up on the airstrip, so you can move into the ranch house anytime after nine," Otis told him.

"Everything is ready to come down so I'll get a load in here tomorrow. I'm really excited to be able to stay out here and see what it looks like at night," Tuck answered.

"It's certainly a beautiful place. There are no lights around to block the stars, and we're sixty seven miles as the crow flies from the border, so you won't have unwanted guests showing up in the middle of the night," Otis told him, "I've made a list of numbers that you might need to call for any questions that you might have. If there are any emergencies that come up, call me immediately and let me know what is happening down here. You never know what might go wrong on a place that is this isolated. Oh, I should tell you that no one is authorized to use that airstrip. If you hear something coming in or taking off out there, call for backup. We've had reports of a couple of incidents lately that have me a little concerned."

"Relax Otis, have a great vacation. I've got this under control," Tuck assured him.

"If I had any doubts, we wouldn't be leaving tomorrow, Tuck. Some of my friends followed your escapades more closely than I have, but the way that you handled yourself in all of the Myrtle Beach stuff was impressive," Otis told him.

"Thanks, Otis, but I am hoping to be bored to tears while you're gone," Tuck said with a smile, not knowing that events were in play that would adversely affect them all in a very short time.

"Let's go back to the house and let me hold that little one. Those women shouldn't have all of the fun," Otis clapped him on the back and headed for the house.

Early the next morning they took Kathryn to the airport and watched until she boarded her flight, then it was off to the Thunder Ranch and a new adventure. Hanna wanted to know all of the stories that Tuck had heard about the ranch's history and asked question after question as Tuck struggled to answer them. They were at the ranch before they knew it, and Tuck enlisted the help of the two ranch hands to get the truck unloaded and Hanna settled with the baby.

"I've got to make my rounds, Hanna. I wish that you could go with me around the place and see how big it is," Tuck told her.

"Julia gave me the number of a girl in McCamey that goes to their church. She's looking for some work, and can stay out here with Emily and me during the week. Maybe I can go with you in a couple of days if she works out," Hanna replied hopefully.

"I sure hope so Babe. Hey, Luke will be down this afternoon. We're going to scout for that Black Panther this evening, how about giving me a call when he gets here," Tuck said.

"You know that I will, but I don't like the idea of you leaving me all day and part of the night on my first day here," Hanna sounded irritated.

"I won't be late tonight; Hanna, and tomorrow I'll spend all day right here with you and Emily. We can make a small tour and pack a little picnic. I know just the spot," Tuck had planned on surprising Hanna with a look at the monkey.

"I'm going to hold you to that promise, Michael Tucker. Now go get your work finished so we can have at least a little of the evening to cuddle," Hanna hugged him and went back into the house.

Tuck's first stop was the tank where the monkey was staying. He took another orange from his bag of fruit and placed it in the crotch of the tree like the last two times, and then walked slowly around the small pond checking for any sign of the big cat. When he cam back to the old tree that the monkey had been in, the orange was gone, but the monkey was nowhere to be seen. Tuck walked back to the ATV and was about to place his rifle in the back seat when his attention was drawn to the roof of the vehicle. Sitting there, eating his orange was the monkey!

"Hey there, little fella," Tuck said quietly and calmly so as not to spook his new found friend, "are you going to ride with me today?"

The monkey held his orange in one hand as he climbed down off of the roof of the ATV to the ground about three feet from Tuck's leg and just looked up at him. Tuck slowly reached into his pack and retrieved a banana, which he just as slowly handed to the monkey. The little animal looked at it for a second, and then took it before scampering off to the waterhole.

"I guess not," Tuck said with a laugh and drove off to the next feeder to scout for sign of the large predator.

Hanna called about two hours later, and Tuck drove back to the ranch house to pick up Luke. They had just finished loading Luke's pack into the ATV when Hanna came out of the house.

"Really? You're just going to come in and leave again without coming in to see me. Both of you get in here right now. I've got coffee made and some soup."

"I guess we had better go in, Luke. Coffee sounds pretty good right about now," Tuck said with a laugh.

Both men followed Hanna into the kitchen and sat at the table while she poured the coffee for them before bringing three bowls of soup to the table.

"So tell me what you saw today, Michael," She said after they asked a blessing on the meal.

"That monkey was on top of the ATV when I finished checking the pond for tracks. He took a banana from my hand and walked back to his tree. That was the darndest thing I've ever seen" Tuck told her.

"I'll bet that monkey was a pet before he got loose. It probably won't take too much to get him to come home," Luke added.

"I don't know about a monkey around here with the baby, Tuck. We need to be careful," Hanna was being cautiously concerned.

"Well, he probably won't be here until Otis gets back, and we'll be in the trailer down there. The monkey won't be in there with us, he'll probably be up here with Otis and Julia," Tuck tried to reassure her.

"Tuck we need to get out of here if we are going to make the high tank and back before dark. I sure don't want to be up there after dark with a black cat that big. Can you imagine the bad luck that could bring?" Luke said with a laugh.

"You men are like little boys!' Hanna declared with a smile, "Go on so you can be back at a reasonable time, and be careful!"

The men rode to the high ground of the water tank where the big jaguar had hidden, stopping every so often to glass the terrain for any sign that the cat was working his territory, but to no avail until they arrived at the wet area just downhill from the holding tank. There were the jaguar's tracks in the soft mud leading toward the cave, and they were on the top of tracks that had been made before the previous night's sparse rain.

"Luke, we might be able to kill this thing right now if we can surprise him in the cave," Tuck said to his friend.

"You don't think the cat heard us coming in that noisy ATV?" Luke asked sarcastically.

"He might have, but the tracks are headed in that direction, not back down hill like he was leaving," Tuck responded as he took his rifle out of the ATV and checked to make certain that a round was in the chamber, "When we get to the other side of the tank, take a look over the edge just to make sure he is not hiding in the water again."

"Well, okay, but you have that rifle ready in case that thing jumps on me!" Luke exclaimed, as he walked over to the edge of the tank and peered in, "Nothing in there but a couple of dead raccoons," He observed, "Let's get to the cave."

Tuck tested the wind direction, which was straight off of their backs. The panther would smell them long before they could get close to the cave.

He whispered to Luke, "Let's idle the ATV back down to the other side of the cave and make a climb with the wind in our faces."

"What's going to stop that cat from running back out here and getting away?" Luke asked.

"There's my Remington 870 in the ATV. You take it and get in that mesquite clump over there. If he comes through here, he will pass within thirty yards of that clump. Just be real quiet so he doesn't see you," Tuck told him.

"Roger that, just give me a second to get set up," Luke told him as he worked the slide on the 870 and loaded a four-aught buck into the chamber. Then he said with a smile, "Here kitty, kitty, kitty, kitty."

Tuck just shook his head and drove the ATV slowly and quietly back down the grade.

The jaguar came out of the small opening in the rock face of the butte, and stretched. He was hungry and thought only of his next kill. Suddenly, he threw up his head and sampled the strong westerly wind as it brought traces of the men's scent to his nostrils. On the other side of the gully that separated him from the road, he saw the ATV moving slowly as Tuck tried to get into a position to surprise the cat. He couldn't know that the jaguar had decided on him for his next meal.

Tuck brought the Polaris to a complete stop and killed the idling engine. He would have to cross a very thick portion of the gully and get to the cat quickly if he wanted to get home by dark. Tuck tightened his Kevlar leggings and started the walk down into the dense brush with all of his senses on alert. Not only did he have to keep an eye pealed for rattlesnakes, but there were other things besides the jaguar that could hurt him in here.

The jaguar had Tuck's scent now and made his fast-paced stalk to within fifty yards of Tuck's position without being seen. He would lie in wait until the human had passed him, and then rush in to seize Tuck from behind and crush his head between his powerful jaws. Tuck was moving slowly past the jaguar at an angle that had shortened the distance between them to thirty yards. The cat could taste the blood in his mouth and his every nerve was focused on making this kill.

Tuck heard the cat as it started its lunge toward him and spun around in a futile effort to defend himself. Just as the massive cat reached a point ten yards from his intended victim, the vicious Mexican fighting bull that had escaped from the buyers when they had taken the rest of them off of the ranch, charged from his thick cover with a crash and a bellow and smashed into the cat as it was in mid-air. The black jaguar let out a hideous scream of rage and pain as the bull hooked him with its needle sharp horns, tossing him again into the air and into a large clump of prickly pear cactus, its thousands of needle like spines penetrating skin at the slightest touch. With a scream, the big cat bolted away from the bull and ran at full speed toward the high tank and Luke's ready shotgun.

Tuck eyed the bull warily which now had its head down and was pawing the ground, throwing dirt over his back. Thinking that this would be a good time to make an exit, Tuck slowly backed around a thick clump of mesquite while the bull was looking in the direction that the cat had run.

"BOOM, BOOM, BOOM" Tuck heard the Remington fire as fast as Luke could pull the slide, and he picked up his pace returning to the ATV. No sooner had he gotten the Polaris turned around than the enraged bull broke the cover of the gully and charged straight at Tuck, who waited until the last minute before hitting the accelerator and passing just in front of the maddened animal.

"Ha Toro!" he exclaimed with a laugh as he opened the throttle and put some distance between them. They would have to deal with it on the way back, but right now Luke might need his help.

Luke was standing next to the tank when Tuck slid around the corner and came to a stop in the front of him.

"What happened? Did you get him?" Tuck asked excitedly.

"That darned thing came around the far side of that tank running like the hounds of hell were on his tail. By the time I got on him with the shotgun, he was already over the fence and in the mesquite so I threw three rounds in there just in case," Luke sounded exasperated.

"That cat almost got me down there, Luke. Just before he was on me, that Mexican bull came out of nowhere and kicked the living crap out of him. The cat ended up in a cactus patch that really lit him up. Right after that, I heard the shotgun," Tuck explained, "That bull is some kind of fired up too. We might have to kill him if he's in the road."

"Well, let's head on back. Maybe he will have left the area. I'm getting to old for much more excitement tonight, but it sure is fun!" Luke laughed.

"Well, you take my rifle and try to angle one up behind that bull's shoulder if we have to shoot him. He's about seven hundred pounds of muscle and will probably take a good bit of killing from what Otis told me," Tuck instructed him as he handed over his Remington 700.

They moved slowly back down the trail until they were close to the head of the gully that the bull called home. Standing broadside to them at two hundred yards was the bull, still slinging dirt over his back and shaking his head from side to side.

"Go ahead and take him, Luke. Stay close to the shoulder but away from the bone," Tuck whispered, expecting Luke to steady the rifle on the windshield frame of the ATV.

Luke just stepped out of the ATV and raised the rifle to his shoulder. The crack of the rifle was almost instantaneous to the move, and Tuck thought that he might have accidentally hit the trigger, but the bull was on his knees with blood pouring from his nose. Immediately following the first shot came the second, and the bull rolled over on his right side and lay still.

"Man that was some good shooting, Luke," Tuck congratulated the older man.

"My dad always taught us that a good rifleman should be able to hit a three inch target with five rounds rapid fire at one hundred yards offhand, if the rifle was up to the task...yours certainly is," Luke replied with a grin as he handed the custom Remington back to Tuck.

Tuck made a call to the house, "Hey Hon, are the hands still on the ranch? Tell them to head up to the high water tank with that lowboy trailer and a tractor. We killed that mean bull that Otis warned us about. We're through up here, but I want to wait for those men just in case they need some help loading it up. Love you too."

"They'll be up here in about twenty minutes. Let's go look at your bull," Tuck said to Luke as he ended the call.

"I feel kind of bad about killing the bull that saved your life, Tuck. I hope we did the right thing," Luke said as they drove to the downed bull.

"That bull would have eventually hurt or killed someone on the ranch, Luke. Otis wanted it gone," Tuck told him, "We've had a pretty good day. Besides that, the winter meat supply is taken care of."

"Are you going to call Manny and tell him about the run in with that cat of his, Tuck," Luke asked.

"He'll be over at the tank battery with his crew tomorrow. I'll drop by in the morning and let him know what has been happening since the hunt. You know, I'll bet he doesn't know that we caught that female cat either," Tuck answered.

"I'd like to have seen his face when that panther jumped out of that tank, but I probably would have messed up my drawers too," Luke laughed.

The panther ran for almost a mile before he stopped to tend his wounds, which included another long tear in his flesh from the bull's horns, and a thousand prickly pear cactus spines that would eventually fester and work themselves out. It would take weeks and could cause enough irritation to the cat that he would be extremely dangerous to any animal or man that happened into him. With his home area compromised so many times in one week, the panther scouted for another place to hunt from, his search bringing him to an area above the airstrip and closer to the ranch house.

CHAPTER 14

"Good morning Senor Tuck," Manny Hernandez called loudly as Tuck pulled up to the jobsite early the next day.

"Hi Manny," Tuck replied as he got out of the ATV, "How are you doing?'

"I want to thank you for taking me on that hunt for the devil cat, Tuck. I have slept better in the past couple of nights than I have in thirty years," Manny told him, "Maria says that it is because I faced my biggest fear and survived, but I told her that God protected me. She said that if I believe that, then I need to thank Him, so I am going to church with her this next Sunday, although I've never been in a Baptist church before."

That's great Manny!" Tuck exclaimed, and then proceeded to tell him about the activities of the day before. "...and I'll bet that cat is still running south!" he finished with a laugh.

"I wish that I could have seen that bull toss him into the cactus," Manny replied to the end of Tuck's story, "By the way Tuck, the men said that they saw some people crossing into the canyon south of us at first light this morning. They might be poachers."

"Thanks Manny, I'll drive over there and check for sign. If it looks like anything, I'll give Warden Ledbetter a call," Tuck responded with a handshake before walking back to the ATV and retrieving his Leupold binoculars. He scanned the face of the bluff in the direction that Manny had indicated, but didn't see any movement. It looked like a trip would be in order.

Tuck drove the half of a mile to the spot that the men had seen the trespassers, and stopped the ATV about one hundred yards short of the canyon mouth. Taking his rifle from the rack on the ATV, Tuck pulled the bolt open to check that it had rounds in the magazine. He also didn't want to give the impression that he was prepared to shoot at trespasser so he left the bolt open.

Working his way slowly through thc slight draw and studying the ground for sign, Tuck finally found a faint impression of one set of boots exactly where Manny's crew had seen the people enter that draw that passed as a canyon out here. It was time to call Chief of Game Wardens Robert Ledbetter for some help.

"Hello Tuck, how can I help you today?" Bob Ledbetter answered the phone after his secretary announced the call from Tuck.

"Good morning, Chief Ledbetter, I've got a situation out here that might involve some poaching, and I was wondering if you could send a man out to help me check it out," Tuck explained.

"It will take about an hour to get someone over there Tuck. If you have a GPS coordinate, we can have a plane fly that area and maybe get a visual," Ledbetter replied.

"I'll have it to you in about three minutes," Tuck told him as he dug through his pack for the Garmin GPS that he carried.

Once the coordinates were reported, Tuck sat in the ATV and waited for the sound of an airplane, which didn't take long to arrive overhead. The plane flew close to the ground and directly over the canyon above the coordinates that Tuck had relayed in, and then started widening the circle of the search. Tuck's phone rang.

"Tuck, the pilot just called in and said that he didn't see anything unusual in the area, but heavy brush is hampering the search so it will probably have to be done on foot. I'm going to have him stay on station until one of my men gets there in about ten minutes...just in case," Bob Ledbetter reported.

Tuck thanked him and drove back to the ranch entrance at the tank battery to wait on the game warden to show up. In just under the ten minutes that Chief Ledbetter had promised, one of the game wardens that had been on the jaguar hunt showed up in his truck. Tuck met him as he parked and got out. It was the taller of the two that had darted the cat, and Tuck remembered that his name was Jeff.

"Hello Jeff thanks for coming to check on this for me," Tuck offered his hand.

"Glad to do it, Tuck. What have we got?" the game warden asked as he took Tuck's hand.

"Some contractor saw people walking into that canyon over there," Tuck pointed in the direction of the draw, "and I thought they might be poaching deer. That's the area that has the muley herd."

"Well, let's go check them out. Maybe they are just hikers from one of the other ranches," Jeff replied.

The men got into the ATV and rode over to the canyon mouth, which was just a point where the valley floor gently rose up into two hills created by hundreds of years of erosion that carved a canyon out of a large bluff. Tuck drove slowly into the dense brush at the canyon mouth until Jeff signaled him to stop. The spotter plane made a pass over them and waved his wings to let them know that he had seen them before leaving the area.

"Let's go from here on foot," The warden said quietly, "We are too close to the border to take chances on hikers being friendly."

Tuck reached into the back of the Polaris and took the Remington 870 from the rack, "For snakes."

"You can't be too careful out here. We have all kinds of snakes, some upright," Jeff told him with a smile, "Let's work about twenty yards apart until we find something; use hand signals from here on."

Tuck nodded as he checked the shotgun and then reached into the box of shells and put five more into his pocket. The men moved slowly up the canyon looking for any sign that others had been through there this morning. After stopping where Tuck had seen the single track in the hard ground, it didn't take long to pick up a trail that had been made by four sets of tracks, all wearing a similar lugged bottom boot. Tuck's gut was telling him that these were not civilians, and he relayed that information to Jeff. They moved more cautiously now climbing the upward sloping floor of the canyon and keeping an eye on the sloping walls for any ambush attempt. After an hour of following the tracks that the makers had not attempted to hide, they came across an old trail that ran from the top of the bluff down to the south and west. The mesquite and cactus that had grown up over the years was freshly broken down and new tracks indicated that a heavy vehicle with lugged tires had picked up the hikers and driven out very recently, probably just before the plane made its pass over the canyon.

"I need to call this in, Tuck, but there is no signal here. Let's get back to the ATV; this is a matter for Homeland now," Jeff told him.

As they fast walked back, Tuck wondered what these people were up to. He knew that there had been incursions by the Mexican military across the border, but didn't remember hearing of one this far in. As Jeff called the report in to Chief Ledbetter, Tuck drove them back to the tank battery and Jeff's truck.

"Tuck, thanks for calling this in. We'll be in touch if anything turns up, and you can probably expect to hear from the feds too," Jeff said as he shook his hand.

"Glad to help, Jeff. If there is anything that I can do for you, please don't hesitate to ask," Tuck said in reply.

"Well, here is one thing. The Chief said to remind you to get your license this week so you can shoot back if you need to," Jeff said with a smile as he got in his truck. Tuck just smiled and waved. The story of Tuck's encounter with the female jaguar would probably be told for the next forty years or as long as Jeff and Chief Ledbetter were around to tell it.

Tuck drove back to the pond where the monkey was staying, determined to make a little more headway with his little friend. As he drove up to the edge of the pond, he shut the engine off and held out an orange in the direction of the tree. In less than thirty seconds, the monkey came down the tree and walked slowly to the ATV and Tuck's out stretched hand. He looked up at Tuck briefly, and then took the orange. Instead of running back to the tree, the monkey sat down and started eating it. Tuck was amazed to say the least.

"Hey little guy, how about riding back to the ranch house with me?" Tuck said to the little primate, not really expecting an answer.

The monkey watched Tuck while it finished the orange, and then extended his hand again. Tuck handed him a banana, which the monkey took and then laid it down beside him before extending his hand again. Tuck was puzzled by this new behavior and reached slowly toward the monkey's outstretched hand with his own. As soon as Tuck touched the end of the monkey's fingers, it made a face that resembled a smile, picked up its banana, and walked slowly back to the tree. Tuck knew that it was only a matter of a few short days before the little guy was back at the ranch house and safety.

His mind now turned to the business of the people that they had tracked that morning. There had to be someone that had some information on border incursions, and Tuck knew just who to call.

"Joel, how are you doing?" He asked when Joel Biggs answered his phone.

"Hey Tuck, this is a surprise. What's up with you?" Joel asked suspiciously.

"Joel, there were some people on the ranch today that seemed to all have military boots on and left overland in a heavy vehicle, a large SUV or something similar, with knobby tires. Is the FBI lurking around down here?" Tuck asked.

There was a second or so delay before Joel answered, "Not that I'm aware of Tuck. Let me get settled in here, and I'll do some checking for you."

"I thought you were in El Paso, Joel. Where are you now?" Tuck asked.

"I'll be in Alpine for a few weeks, Tuck. I'm training with the Border Patrol over here for some joint mission preparation, and then it is back to El Paso," Joel made no mention about the kidnapping of Noah Escobar since there was an absolute news blackout on the event.

"Well, ask around for me there also. Those guys should know if any Mexican military has crossed over, even if they can't do anything about it," Tuck replied, "I'll call you if I see them again."

"Okay Tuck, I'll talk to you soon," Joel ended the call.

Tuck spent the rest of the day close to the ranch house making certain that the two ranch hands stayed busy at the chores that Otis had left for them, and taking the time to get in the house to play with Emily as much as he could.

"Tuck, that girl Rosa's mother said she could stay during the week and help with the baby, but you need to go get her," Hanna told him toward mid-afternoon.

"Why don't we both go, Hanna? I'd feel a lot better if you were with me when I pick her up. Somehow it doesn't feel right for me to go alone," Tuck practically begged.

"You are absolutely right, Michael. I'll wrap up Emily, and we'll head right out," Hanna replied and gave him a big hug.

Joel called back as they were leaving, "Tuck, I've got some news that might explain your trespassers. A small plane left Mexico about two weeks ago with what we believe were ISIS terrorists onboard. That plane went down to the south of you, but we found only one person in the wreckage and can't account for the other four men. They've probably left your area, but exercise caution if you see anyone out there that isn't supposed to be there."

Tuck had the feeling that Joel wasn't being quite truthful with him but answered, "Thanks for the heads up, Joel. I'll call if I see anything resembling a Muslim on the ranch."

After the call ended, he turned to Hanna, "It just gets better and better, love. Now it appears that not all of the illegals coming across the border are coming for peaceful purposes. It shouldn't affect us though."

CHAPTER 15

The next week seemed to fly by with Hanna now able to take a couple of hours a day to ride the ranch with Tuck. He introduced her to the monkey and although the little animal was skittish at first, by the second day he was taking food from Hanna's hand. On the third trip out, Hanna got out of the ATV and sat on the ground with the fruit in her hand. Tuck just watched in amazement as the monkey walked over to Hanna, and then climbed into her lap where he stayed while he ate the orange that she handed to him. Hanna talked softly to the monkey the whole time, but didn't make any effort to touch him. When he had finished the orange, the little primate reached up and touched her gently on the cheek before going to the ATV where Tuck sat, and held his hand out for a banana. As soon as Tuck handed it to him, the monkey went back to Hanna's lap and laid his head against her chest for just a few seconds before heading back to his tree.

"Did you see that Michael? The monkey likes me!" Hanna exclaimed.

"I think that he sees you as a mother image," Tuck responded, "But it was kind of interesting to watch. Maybe you can coax him to come to the house with us."

"Maybe, but I'm still concerned about him being around the baby," Hanna replied, "I need to get back and check on Emily. Are you still going to go out tonight?"

"I need to check on the deer herds tonight around the feeders. Do you want to come with me?" Tuck asked hopefully.

"No, that wouldn't be fair to Rosa, and it won't be fair to Emily and me if you don't at least spend the afternoon at home since you are going to be late getting in tonight," Hanna was smiling, but she was also serious, a fact that was not lost on Michael Tucker.

"That sounds like a good idea, Hanna. I don't need to leave until just before dark so maybe we can grill some of the steaks off of that bull this afternoon," Tuck suggested.

"You have a date Mr. Tucker," Hanna replied as she leaned across the ATV console and gave him a kiss.

Tuck spent the rest of the morning cutting up a hindquarter of the bull that was hanging in a small walk in cooler, and coming up with two huge steaks for the grill that afternoon. He was looking forward to having this time with his girls, and the thoughts of the trouble that had plagued them from the start of their marriage seemed like a distant bad dream. Later that day, Tuck prepared for a late night's work by packing some heavier clothes in hopes of combating the cool air of the west Texas night, and cleaning the rifle and shotgun before returning them to their places in the ATV.

"What time are you going to be home, Michael?" Hanna asked sweetly as she came out to see him off.

"I'm thinking about ten o'clock Hanna," Tuck replied, "I want to see what's hanging around the feeders after the sun goes down."

"Be careful out there and call me if you're going to be late so I don't worry," Hanna replied.

"I will, but don't worry about me if I don't call right at ten. The signal is really weak out to the west of the house," Tuck told her as he gave his wife a big hug before heading off to try and get a good count of the night's herd activities.

Driving slowly along the trail to the west end of the ranch, Tuck let the Polaris idle along so that the engine noise wouldn't spook any of the wildlife that he hoped to see on the night scouting foray. Occasionally he threw the blue beam of the Q-light across an opening in the mesquite and interrupted deer in their night feeding cycle. Shutting the ATV down after driving about two miles from the ranch house, He just sat there in the cool darkness, and looked at the millions of stars that seemed so close that he could reach out and touch them. As he turned his head toward the southeast, he thought that he saw a shimmer of yellow light in one of the deep draws that had been eroded into the steep butte. Tuck looked away for a second, and then looked back with just the edge of his vision, an old trick that his father had taught him. There it was; a small campfire that signaled the presence of someone else in this remote part of the ranch, someone that obviously was not supposed to be here.

He took the Leupold Binoculars out of his pack and scanned the area of the draw. It didn't take long before the fire backlit at least two figures close to the fire. Tuck continued to observe the area as he weighed his options. Luke Moffet was at least one hundred miles away, and there was almost no chance of getting a sheriff's deputy to respond to what was for now just a simple trespass charge. If he put the sneak on those people and they were part of the group that Joel warned him about, they might have a forward sentry posted that could put him in grave danger. His second sense was running high alert flags, so he decided to call the location in and wait for backup, if he could get any, but who to call?

With his cell phone showing only one signal bar, he decided to call Joel Biggs who he hoped was still in Alpine with a group of Border Patrol agents. Joel's phone rang twice before the FBI agent answered, "Hello Tuck, what's going on?"

"Joel, I'm sitting near the old airstrip on the Thunder Ranch and watching some activity up in one of the draws about a half a mile from me. There are at least two people around a campfire, maybe more. You were the only one that I thought might be interested," Tuck replied quietly into the phone.

Joel was silent for a minute before answering, "Tuck, I've got two special ops guys with me here, and we can be there in about an hour, give or take a few minutes. Get yourself into a hide of some sort and keep an eye on them for me."

"Can do Joel, I have one question though. Don't you think that a plane is liable to spook these guys if they are ISIS?" Tuck asked.

"We won't be landing in a plane. I'll text a signal when we drop."

"Copy that Joel. I'll be standing by," Tuck ended the call.

"Well, nothing to do but wait now," Tuck thought to himself as he checked his rifle and got his pack ready for the climb. After making certain that his gear was safely out of sight of any night vision gear, he decided to call Hanna and let her know that he would be late getting in.

"Hi hon," Tuck spoke softly after Hanna answered her phone, "I'm going to be late getting back tonight, and didn't want you to worry."

"What going on Michael?" Hanna asked with a little concern in her voice, "Do I need to come and get you in the other ATV?"

"No, everything is fine. There is some activity that needs to be checked before I come in is all. It's nothing to worry about. How is Emily?" He answered quietly.

"Emily is fine Michael. What do you mean by 'activity'? I thought that we were alone out here," Hanna sounded worried.

"Well, we are supposed to be, but there is someone up one of the hidden draws. I've called Joel Biggs, and he will be out here to investigate in about an hour. I should be home right after that. I promise," Tuck tried to sound reassuring. Right now, it was starting to feel like making the call to Hanna might not have been the right thing to do.

"Michael Tucker, you are not to take any unnecessary risks. Do you hear me?" Hanna put her foot firmly down."

"Loud and clear, Love, loud and clear. I'll call before I head back," He tried to get Hanna settled down.

"If I don't hear from you in two hours, I am coming out there. Rosa can take care of the baby," Hanna proclaimed.

"Don't come out here, Hanna. I'm serious now. I'll call as soon as I'm on the way in"

"Two hours Michael and I mean it," Hanna ended the call.

Hanna waited a few minutes, and then placed a call to Luke Moffet, "Luke, this is Hanna Tucker. There is something going on down here, and I didn't know who to call besides you."

"Hello Hanna, tell me what's wrong. Maybe I can help," Luke replied, and then listened while Hanna filled him in on Tuck's situation.

"Let me tell Mary, and then I'm on the way down. Give me about an hour and a half to get there," Luke replied.

"Luke, I hate to ask you to drive down this late, but I sure do appreciate it," Hanna said.

"Just have the coffee on when I get there, Hanna, and don't worry. Tuck can take care of himself," Luke answered and then ended the call.

Hanna was relieved that Luke was coming down. While she waited to hear from Tuck and for Luke's arrival, she went to the gun safe and removed her 6.5x55 Swedish Mauser that had already saved Tuck's life on one occasion. She loaded the magazine with five 140-grain Hornady boat tails and made certain that the optics were clean…just in case.

The light buzz of Tuck's cell phone signaled a text message from Joel. Tuck returned to the ATV and waited. Soon he heard the sound of a light plane as it crossed over the ranch and faded into the distance. Suddenly, out of the night sky came three men in black para-gliders, expertly dropping to the ground within one hundred feet of Tuck's position. One of the men dropped his chute and walked briskly to Tuck.

"Hey Tuck, we made it with time to spare. Where are these people?" Joel asked as he handed Tuck a set of night vision optics.

"Right up there near the crest of that butte, Joel," Tuck pointed in the direction of the draw.

The men rolled the chutes up and stashed them in the ATV, and then shouldered their packs and suppressed M-4 carbines. With Tuck in the lead, they moved quickly and quietly across the thorny mesquite and cactus covered wash and headed in the general direction of the draw. When they had covered roughly a quarter of a mile through the brush and cactus, Joel silently signaled for his group to spread out and keep an eye peeled for a security perimeter while he and Tuck moved slowly and silently straight up the rise in the butte. That would bring them to some large rocks within one hundred yards of the campfire that was burning just inside a cover of heavy mesquite.

When they arrived at the rock cover, Tuck and Joel decided to rely on their eyes and instincts over the value of the night vision glasses and carefully removed them before stepping out and continuing their advance. The fire was making hot spots in their vision with them on, and they didn't want to risk not being able to see into the camp when the opportunity presented itself. Hopefully, these were just hikers ignorant of the fact that they were trespassing, but Tuck had learned that it didn't pay to let your guard down for a second. Joel signaled for them to hold position, so Tuck raised his binoculars slowly to scout the camp entrance. It only took a very short second for him to realize that the occupants of the camp were not in it, and the fire was a diversion!

As he turned to Joel Biggs and gave him a neck chopping signal to abort, a flash bang grenade went off in front of them, blinding Joel who was looking toward the fire. Tuck was knocked backward by the concussion of the blast but uninjured. Suddenly the air was filled with the ragged sound of an AK-47 on full auto and the shriek of the rounds as they tore through the air over their heads and into the rocks surrounding them.

"Joel, roll to your left and get behind that rock!" Tuck shouted to his temporarily blinded comrade. He quickly fired two shots as fast as he could work the bolt on the 700 Remington at the muzzle blast of the AK, and then sprinted to the rock that Joel was now crouched behind.

"Are you hit?" Tuck shouted above the noise of a second AK-47 that had opened on their position.

"No, but I've got bright lights going off in my eyes. Take my M-4 and see if you can't quiet one of those guys down," Joel answered as he handed Tuck the rifle.

Tuck traded weapons with Joel and started to target the closest enemy when the firing suddenly went silent. The two other agents appeared with their M-4s held at the ready, and on the ground midway between Tuck and the fire were the bodies of the two men that had pinned them down.

"Come on Joel, your team is here," Tuck said as he got hold of Joel's arm and helped him to his feet.

By the time that they reached the camp, Joel's vision had cleared, and he talked to his men about the mission. Tuck looked through the pile of gear on the floor of the small tent and realized that there were more supplies than necessary for the two men outside.

"We've got a problem guys," Tuck said as he straightened up, "There are at least two more of these guys out here, and we need to find them."

"We might have more of a problem than that sir," One of the agents had turned the closest of the dead men over to reveal the swarthy complexion of what looked like a Middle Eastern background in the firelight. He was also wearing the black headdress of the ISIS fighters. A look at the second body revealed the same characteristics.

"ISIS terrorists on a ranch smack dab in the middle of Texas. Who is going to give a 'fair and balanced' report on this, I wonder?" Joel said as he examined the corpses, "I'm going to have a hard time explaining how we killed two Islamic terrorists in Texas when they don't officially exist."

"Joel, I've got to get to the ranch house. Hanna is down there with the baby and a housekeeper. They could be in danger," Tuck looked at his cell phone for some glimmer of a signal so that he could warn Hanna, but there was nothing.

"You men stay here and secure this area while Tuck and I head to the house. If you hear shots fired try to get on up to the butte top and phone it in," Joel spoke to the other men, "Come on Tuck, let's get back to the ATV, and make a run for the house."

They had covered maybe fifty yards when the distant sound of full auto gunfire came from the direction of the ranch house followed by the sharper reports of a rifle and the steady popping of a handgun.

"They're at the house!" Tuck shouted to Joel as he started to half sprint and half slide down the steep terrain toward the ATV. Oblivious to the thorns that stabbed at him and scratched his hands and face, Tuck barreled on through the dense cover with Joel directly behind. All that he could think about was Hanna and Emily being butchered by these cowardly ISIS dogs, and a blind rage drove him on.

After what seemed like an eternity they arrived at the ATV, and just as they were slinging their gear into the back seat, Tuck's cell phone rang, it was Hanna's phone, "MICHAEL, I need you at the house please hurry!" Hanna was crying.

"Hanna, what happened? Are you and Emily alright?" Tuck was afraid of the answer.

"We are fine Michael, but Luke has been shot, and I don't think he is going to make it," Hanna replied sobbing.

"Luke? Luke was there?" Tuck could hardly get the words out.

"Just hurry Michael, please hurry!" Hanna exclaimed and ended the call.

Tuck had the Polaris screaming as they covered the trail to the ranch house in record time. As they slid up to the front door, they saw the bodies of two more terrorists lying on the sidewalk.

Tuck ran past the bodies and into the house looking for Hanna and Luke while Joel knelt down and checked the men's pulses.

"I'm in the living room Michael. Hurry up please," Hanna's voice shouted to them.

Luke was lying on the couch with a towel folded up on his lower right chest and another wrapped around his right thigh to control the bleeding. His skin was a sickly gray from loss of blood, but his eyes were open.

"One of those Arabs shot me Tuck!" Luke offered weakly, "I must have lost my touch."

"Don't try to speak Luke. We are going to get you some help." Tuck said gently as he knelt beside the couch and placed his hand over the towel to help apply pressure to the chest wound. He looked around at Joel who just nodded, and then headed for the door to call for an air-evac.

"They shot me as I got out of my truck, Tuck. I got off a magazine, but didn't hit one. It was just the grace of God that more of those rounds didn't hit me. Hanna shot them both while they were concentrating on me. She sure is fast with that rifle," Luke smiled weakly then added before he lost consciousness, "Can you give Mary a call, and tell her that I will probably be a little late getting home?"

"We'll take care of it my friend," Tuck spoke softly to Luke who was just barely breathing.

"Michael, who were those people?" Hanna asked. She was visibly shaken but had the presence of mind to tend Luke's wounds in spite of her condition.

"We think that they may have been ISIS terrorists, Hanna. At least that is what Joel said might be coming out of Mexico," Tuck replied still holding pressure on Luke's chest wound. The older man was breathing in wheezes now, and Tuck knew that he wouldn't last much longer with out medical treatment, which was impossible to get in this remote area, "Where are Emily and Rosa?"

"Rosa hid with Emily when the shooting started. They are in the bedroom now. Rosa is shaken up, but both are fine. Michael, I killed two men tonight. I just killed them as if I would shoot coyotes when I saw them attacking Luke. I can't stop shaking," Hanna said to him and started crying.

"Sometimes I wish that I could cry over those kinds of things, Hanna. You're lucky in that respect. It will be all right in a few days. These men were dogs that needed killing so don't beat yourself up over it," Tuck did the best that he could do to comfort her without leaving Luke's side, "I think that you should call Mary and tell her what has happened. Her husband is a hero; she needs to know that. Tell her that we will call her when we know where they will take him for treatment."

Tuck was suddenly surprised at the sound of a big helicopter coming from the direction of the butte as Joel ran back into the room.

"We had a chopper for evac sitting one butte over, Tuck. They have a medic on board and will be in the yard shortly. How is Luke doing?" Joel asked.

"It will be close, but this is a tough old nut. He might just make it now," Tuck almost breathed a sigh of relief for his friend.

Within five minutes, Luke had been sedated, had an I.V. in his arm, and a medic was getting him ready for flight. Tuck stood with his arms around Hanna while they prepped Luke.

"Is he going to make it?" Tuck asked the medic.

"I think that your friend will be just fine. Those Full Metal Jacket bullets passed right through without much tissue damage. We'll have to wait for x-rays, but I think that the chest wound might have missed his lung. I'm getting some plasma into him, and he is stabilizing, so let's load him up," The medic replied with a smile.

"That's great news guys. Joel is there anyway that you can tell me where they are going to take Luke. I have to tell his wife where to meet him," Tuck asked.

"We are going to Fort Bliss, but I'll make arrangements to fly to Odessa and pick her up. She should be with him when he wakes up," Joel replied. Then in a worried tone, "By the way, there will probably be a hearing about tonight's events. I'll keep you posted,"

Tuck shook Joel's hand and Hanna came over to give him a hug, "Thanks for taking care of Michael, Joel. It seems that we didn't leave all of our friends in Myrtle Beach after all."

Joel just gave her a smile and left with the stretcher crew.

"Hanna, let's get Emily out of here for a few days. I've made a friend whose wife works at the Hilton in Odessa. I think we can get a good rate on a room," Tuck said as he leaned over to give his wife a kiss, "Besides, this place will be swarming with feds for the next week or so anyway."

"I think that is a wonderful idea Michael. Go get your things packed. I can be ready in about thirty minutes," Hanna gave him another kiss and a squeeze before leaving the room.

Tuck walked over to the door and looked at the place where the bodies of the terrorists had lain. As he looked at the bloodstained concrete of the walkway, he remembered what Harry Albright had told him, "Son, Psalm 91 is God's shield for those that believe, and sometimes in the course of your duties in law enforcement, you will need to be that shield for others."

He wondered how he would make Hanna see that she had performed that same service by saving Luke's life and taking the lives of the men that would have killed her, and all that she held dear.

"That will wait for another time," Tuck thought as he turned to collect his gear from the ATV.

As he returned to the house, he looked again at the still wet patches of blood on the ground. Hurrying inside, Tuck found some cotton swabs and two sandwich bags, and then walked back to the bloodstains where he bent down to take samples of each one with the swabs before putting them in individual bags.

"What are you doing, Michael?" Hanna asked as she walked up behind him carrying Emily.

"I'm just acting on a hunch, babe," Tuck responded as he straightened up with the bags held in his hand, "Give me a second to throw some jeans and underwear in a bag, and we'll get out of here. Oh, have you told Rosa where we are going?"

"No, not yet, she's really shaken up. Here, take Emily and I'll run back in and get the bag that I've packed for you," Hanna answered.

"Well, don't say anything to her about the Hilton. The less people that know where we are, the better I'll sleep," Tuck said as they shifted Emily into his arms.

"Okay Michael, I know how you get those weird feelings about things. We'll drop Rosa off at her mother's on the way back to Odessa," Hanna kissed him on the cheek and returned inside.

"Daddy's hoping he's wrong little one," Tuck said softly to Emily, who was looking up at him with her big blue eyes, "but I don't think that I am."

After they dropped Rosa off with her mother, Hanna said to Tuck, "Michael, everyone in McCamey is going to know about this in a few hours. We need to call Maggie O'Brien so she can get a jump on the other news outfits, although it would be par for the course if they didn't report on it."

"I think that is a good idea, Hanna. Maggie will probably want to lead that investigation herself, and it would be good to see a friendly face from back home," Tuck replied.

Hanna dialed the number for Maggie that was in her phone and waited for several rings before a very sleepy voice answered, "Hello, this is Margaret O'Brien,"

"Hello Maggie. This is Hanna Tucker, and I am calling to give you the first shot at reporting on an ISIS attack on US soil!" Hanna was straight to the point.

"Hanna?" Maggie was suddenly very alert, "What in the world is going on? ISIS? Where? Are you and Tuck okay?"

"We're fine, Maggie. But there has been an attack on the ranch that we are on, and I thought that you would like an exclusive, eye-witness report," Hanna replied.

Maggie was now awake and all business, “Hanna, is this a good number for you? I’m going to be very busy for the next half an hour or so, and then I will call you back. Is that okay?”

“Certainly Maggie, we will be in Odessa at the Hilton in about thirty minutes, but I will stay up for your call…not that I could sleep anyway,” Hanna replied.

When Hanna hung up Tuck said, “I’m going to call Otis after we get to the hotel, hon. He needs to know what’s happening down here, and he probably won’t be very happy to learn that the ranch was being used as a base of operations for that terror cell. I just can’t believe that we didn’t see them sooner.”

Hanna was silent for a minute, and then she responded, “Maybe they didn’t want to be seen until tonight, Michael. I don’t have your instincts, but after what we’ve been through, the timing of the attack seems suspicious to me. What do you think?

“I think that I married an extremely smart lady. That’s what I think. But let’s not talk anymore about this until we get out of the truck,” Tuck said as he reached over to give her hand a gentle squeeze, “By the way, have you got a piece of paper on you? I memorized the serial number on one of the AKs up in the cave and need to write it down.”

Hanna just stared at him for a long couple of seconds before replying, “How do you manage to do that? I mean how can you remember anything with all that stuff going on around you?”

“I don’t really know, but it just seems like whenever there is a lot of activity around me, I’m able to stay focused, I guess,” Tuck answered as Hanna scribbled the number that he gave her, “Keep that safe, hon. I’m going to have some friends check it out for me tomorrow.

It was late when they arrived at the Hilton, but their friend had arranged a suite for them on the top floor facing the parking lot like Tuck requested. Even though they checked in on the drivers licensees and a credit card that Special Agent Morris had given them, Tuck wanted to be able to look into the parking lot during the night, just in case that someone might know that they were here.

The call to Otis was short and to the point, "Otis, this is Tuck. There has been some trouble in the form of gun fire at the ranch, and I thought you should know about it."

"My God, Tuck! What happened? Was anyone hurt?" Otis asked in a shocked tone.

"Luke Moffett is shot but they expect him to live. Four men are dead, and we think they may have been an ISIS sleeper cell that was camped out in the old Indian caves," Tuck told him without emotion.

"I think that Julia and I need to fly back home, Tuck. I can be there in two days from here," Otis offered.

"It will probably be best if you folks stay put up there just in case those men were after you, although I don't think that was the case," Tuck told him without volunteering his thoughts on the matter.

"Very well Tuck. Call me with details as this unfolds, and let me know if I need to come home," Otis said sounding relieved that he wasn't needed just yet.

"Yes sir, I'll call daily with news as I get it," Tuck promised and ended the call.

"Hanna, I'm going to Wal-Mart for a couple of burner phones. Don't let anyone in the room until I get back," Tuck told her when he had hung up from Otis.

Hanna gave him a big hug and said, "Be careful!"

Tuck just smiled at her and left the room, taking the stairway to the lobby rather than ride the elevator. After tonight, he didn't trust anyone or anything except for one person, Shaun O'Brien, and it was time to give the big man a call.

Hanna's cell phone rang about ten minutes after Tuck left the room. It was Maggie O'Brien returning Hanna's call to get more information, and to let Hanna know when she would be in Odessa.

"Hello Maggie," Hanna answered her phone.

"Hi Hanna, I'm catching the red-eye out from New York and will be there in about six hours. We've got a room at the Hilton so we can talk in the morning. How are you holding up?' Maggie's concern was genuine.

"Maggie, my phone is not secure so I can't really tell you anything yet, but I'm going to call you back in about an hour, okay?" Hanna told her.

"That should work out fine, Hanna. I'll have some time to kill anyway," Maggie ended the call. She had scrambled the local Fox News affiliate when Hanna had given her the tip about the attack. Now there was very little to do until she could get her feet on the ground at the Thunder Ranch. Hanna's call could fill her in on important information that her people could not know, but for now, she was busy getting to her flight.

Emily was fussy because her sleep schedule had been interrupted, so Hanna lay down on the king sized bed next to the baby and nursed her. Both of his girls were sound asleep when Tuck returned with the phones. He smiled as he leaned over and kissed Hanna softly on the cheek before taking his new burner phone into the bathroom to make the call to Shaun.

"Michael Tucker, this is a surprise. Especially since it is very early in the morning here. What's wrong?" Shaun answered his phone on the second ring sounding as if he had been wide-awake before the call.

"I'm sorry to bother you Shaun, but I've got a problem that I need your expertise with," Tuck replied, and he slowly filled Shaun O'Brien in on the attack at the ranch, "That's why I want to send you these blood samples to confirm my suspicions about these men's backgrounds. There isn't anyone else that I can trust to run the tests or that has your access."

"Send them down Tuck. I would suggest Fed-Ex next day air, and I will get the tests run as soon as they arrive. You should know that we thwarted an attempt on Bob and Abigail a couple of days ago also, so if your suspicions are what I think they are, I would be surprised if they were right," Shaun told him.

"Are they alright?" Tuck asked with concern in his voice.

"Yes, and I sent a not so subtle message back that this wasn't going to be tolerated anymore. Hopefully, they were able to read it correctly which is why I think something else is in play," Shaun answered.

Tuck knew that if Shaun sent a message to Washington, there were probably body parts involved so he didn't want to know the details.

"Thanks Shaun, I'll get these out the first thing in the morning, and please don't tell Bob about this until we're certain. I don't want him worried for no reason if it turns out that I'm wrong," Tuck responded.

"Whatever you say Tuck. I'll call you on this number as soon as the package arrives," Shaun ended the call.

Hanna woke up as Tuck came back into the room, "How long was I asleep Michael?" she asked groggily.

"Not long, maybe thirty minutes," Tuck answered.

"Did you get the phones; Maggie is expecting a call from me."

"Yours is on the desk, hon," Tuck answered, "I'm going to lie down for a bit while you call."

Tuck carefully moved Emily to the crook of his arm and closed his eyes. Before he drifted off to sleep, he wondered how long he could keep her safe.

CHAPTER 16

Early the next morning, Tuck went to the lobby for breakfast just as Maggie O'Brien was checking in.

"Tuck!" she exclaimed, "How good it is to see you,"

"Hi Maggie," Tuck answered, uncomfortable with the hug that he got, and the attention that the beautiful, and now well known, Maggie O'Brien was drawing to them, "It's good to see you too,"

"Is Hanna coming down?" Maggie asked.

Tuck took her by the arm and led her away from the desk, "We aren't checked in under our names, Maggie. It looks like this might not be what we thought last night, but I won't know for a couple of days. Hanna said to give her about ten minutes to get ready. I think that she knew you would be here this morning."

"Yeah, we talked last night. She said that you were asleep with the baby. Let's go have a cup of coffee while we wait for her," She said as she took Tuck's arm and led him to the breakfast bar. Hanna joined them with Emily about ten minutes later, and it was like old home week as the women hugged like long lost sisters.

Tuck excused himself, got up to leave, and kissed both Hanna and Emily on the tops of their heads, "I've got a ton of things to do this morning, ladies. Hanna, if you need me, just call on the new phone."

"I will Michael, don't be gone too long," Hanna returned the kiss.

"Just a couple of errands, and I'll be back," Tuck promised.

"I'm going to have some questions for you also, Tuck. Will you be able to take me to the ranch when you return?" Maggie asked.

Tuck looked helplessly at Hanna who replied for him, "Michael would be happy to Maggie. We both want this to be over with as soon as possible."

Tuck just nodded his assent and left the women to their talk. His first priority would be to find a Fed-Ex location and get the samples off to Shaun, and his second was to call the owner of the gun shop where he had met Luke. He was certain from what Luke had told him, that this was the man to find out where that AK-47 had come from.

As Tuck walked into the gun shop, he was immediately questioned by a group of men sitting around a table just inside the doorway of the small shop.

"Hello Tuck. We heard about what happened last night down on the ranch. How is Luke? Did you kill those terrorists?" all of them started asking questions at one time.

"I haven't heard any news on Luke, although I was told that he was going to make it. No, I didn't kill any of those men, although I tried to. We were engaging the first group when the attack on the house happened. That's all I know," Tuck was uncomfortable so he made his response brief.

He turned to the owner who was standing behind the counter listening to the conversation, "I have something here that needs to be checked out in a very discreet way. Do you think that you can help?"

He took the paper with the serial number of the AK from his pocket and handed it across the counter.

"I think I know just the man for this job. Is that number off of what I think it is?" He asked.

Not wanting to give away too much to the men that were hanging on every word, Tuck simply said, "Chinese, select fire."

The owner looked him in the eye for a second, and then put the paper in his pocket with a nod, "Take one of my cards and call me tomorrow evening. I'll have something for you then. How bad was Luke hurt?"

"He took two rounds, one in the upper right chest and one in the leg close to the femoral artery, but neither one hit anything major. The Feds had a chopper on the next ridge, and that saved his life. I owe him a lot. If he hadn't driven down, they would have killed my wife and baby along with the nanny before we could have gotten to them," Tuck told him with no emotion in his voice, but anger in his eyes.

"Luke is a special friend of ours, and we heard how your wife managed to get the drop on those bastards before they could kill him. She must be quite a young woman. What was she shooting, anyway?" The storeowner asked.

"She used her 6.5x55 Swede that her Dad built for her. You know, she saved my life with the same rifle when a cougar tried to jump on my head," Tuck answered.

The owner walked over to the ammo rack and took two boxes of 140-grain Hornady 6.5x55 ammo, which he gave to Tuck.

"Tell her that I would like to supply her ammunition for helping Luke. BTW, I have something for you as well," He said as he handed Tuck a box and leaned in to whisper, "Open that when you get in the truck. It's a personal piece that might help you out. Bring it back when you are finished."

Tuck thanked him, said goodbye to the men and the dogs, and then got in the truck to return to the hotel. As soon as he drove away from the gun shop, he pulled the flaps up on the box to reveal a new Kimber Ultra Carry II in one of Luke's holsters. If his hunch turned out to be correct, it would be put to good use!

Hanna insisted on riding back down to the ranch with Tuck and Maggie and soon overcame Tuck's objections. With Emily in the car bed beside her in the back seat of the truck, she filled Maggie in on the events at the house while Tuck told her about the cave incident.

"Tuck, do you think that these were really ISIS terrorists?" Maggie O'Brien asked after they finished telling their story.

"Maggie, I'm waiting on your dad to tell me who they were. I've sent blood samples to him, and he should have them today. I wouldn't put that in your report," Tuck replied.

"Why would you send samples to Dad, Tuck? Do you think that this had something to do with you and Hanna?" Maggie had a shocked tone in her voice.

"Maggie, there were two more attempts on our lives after we left Myrtle Beach, both were thwarted. I really can't rule out that this was also a covert operation that was supposed to look like a terrorist raid on a small ranch, although I would like to think that all of that was behind us now," Tuck told her.

Tuck pulled off of the feeder road unto a rough access road that led to the Thunder Ranch. When they arrived at the last gate, they were stopped by an FBI agent and a county sheriff's deputy. Tuck talked to them briefly, and Maggie showed her credentials before they were allowed to pass.

When they pulled up to the ranch house, Joel Biggs walked over to the truck, "Hello Tuck... Hanna. I didn't expect you to be here this morning, but I have good news about Luke. He's stable, and it looks like he'll be up and about in a week or so. We've taken care of all the arrangements for Mary also."

"Hi Joel, that is great news! You remember Maggie, don't you? She's got the lead on the story, so I brought her along with us," Tuck said as he shook hands with his friend.

"Hi Maggie, of course I remember you. How is the new gig going with Fox?" Joel asked as he shook her hand.

"Hi again Joel," Maggie responded, "Work is great but I wish we could have met under more pleasant circumstances."

"Me too Maggie, let me show you where your people are set up," Joel answered and walked away from Tuck and Hanna with Maggie in tow.

"Well, how about that!" Tuck exclaimed to Hanna, "I think old Joel might have a thing for that red haired reporter."

Hanna just gave him a smile and said, "I'm going to wait in the truck with Emily unless I'm needed, Michael. All of a sudden I'm not feeling so well."

Tuck knew that killing those men would have an affect on Hanna eventually, so he helped her gently back into the truck, "I'll come back over and check on you in a few minutes Hon; you just focus on something other than last night."

"I just feel shaky when I think about it now. I'll be all right in a little while," She answered weakly.

Tuck remembered his first kill and the emotions that he had experienced for several days afterward. He also remembered when he stopped counting and envied Hanna for being able to feel remorse even though the kill was justified.

Joel intercepted Tuck as he walked around to the front of the ranch house where the bodies had lain, "Hey Tuck, I've got a team up near the camp that I have to check on. Do you want to come along?"

"Sure Joel, but I thought you were going to follow Maggie around like a love sick puppy today," He answered with a big grin, "I've got to tell Hanna that I'm going, just give me a minute."

Joel's face turned red before he responded to Tuck's dig, "Well, she's riding up with us too. Go ahead and let Hanna know, I'll wait for you."

Tuck walked back to the truck and told Hanna that they were going up to the terrorist's camp and that he would be back shortly. He then sprinted back to where Joel was waiting.

Tuck laughed at his friend as they made their way to the black GMC Yukon that was to take them within walking distance of the cave area. Maggie was already in the front seat with the agent that was going to drive them, and the Fox News camera truck was parked behind.

"Maggie, can you do me a favor and not mention Hanna and me by name in this report? We really don't need the publicity right now," Tuck asked.

"Well, I never reveal a source, Tuck. I'll keep the focus on Agent Biggs and his heroic efforts to save the people on the ranch from the terrorist attack. Is that all right with you, Agent Biggs?" Maggie replied with a smile.

"Of course Maggie, but only if you call me Joel," Joel answered while Tuck just rolled his eyes.

Maggie just laughed and said, "I thought it would be...Joel"

"I should warn you to be on the lookout for rattlesnakes as we climb to the terrorist's camp, also the mesquite thorns, cactus, and sharp rocks," Tuck told her.

"Oh, I'm sure that 'Joel' will protect me, won't you Agent Biggs?" Maggie responded with a big smile.

"I'll do my best Ma'am," Joel said in his best imitation of John Wayne to the laughter of everyone in the car.

The climb to the camp at the head of the secluded draw was uneventful however, and they were met by a dozen agents and sheriff's deputies that were combing through the camp and surrounding area for evidence. Maggie got her camera crew set up and started filming an interview with Joel as the spokesman for the FBI. Tuck was surprised at the details that weren't mentioned by Joel, and wondered if Maggie caught the omissions also. If she did, she didn't let it affect her, and the report went out live, flawlessly.

"When do you have to go back, Maggie?" Joel asked when the filming was finished.

"I've got a flight out in the morning Joel, why do you ask?"

"Tuck tells me that they've got a pretty good menu at the hotel, and I was wondering if I could talk you into dinner tonight," Joel answered with a grin.

"Why Agent Biggs, are you hitting on me?" Maggie asked in her best Southern Belle imitation.

"I certainly am, Maggie, and I've been meaning to ever since we met in Myrtle Beach," Joel responded with a laugh.

"Joel, your persistence has paid off, but I want some good Mexican food while I'm out here. Why don't you pick me up at the hotel at seven sharp and we'll find a cozy place to eat. I'm going back with the camera crew; I'll see you boys at the ranch house," Maggie gave them a big smile and then turned to Tuck, "I'll check on Hanna when I get back there. I know this has to be hard on her."

"Thanks Maggie. I appreciate it.' Tuck answered.

"Okay Tuck, I need the name of a good Mexican restaurant, and I need it now!" Joel said to Tuck in desperation.

Tuck laughed at Joel and replied, "There is a real fancy one called Ajuua's that John and Louise took us to right after we got here. It has a lot of class and some really interesting decorations, not that you will be able to see any of it."

"I owe you Tuck. These guys have this under control; let's get back down to the ranch house," Joel said as he led the way back to the SUV.

"Joel, is there anything that you're not telling me about these guys?' Tuck asked him as they rode back to the ranch house.

"Tuck, there is such a lid on this crap that I couldn't tell you what I wasn't telling you. If you understand what I'm getting at," Joel answered, "Besides, I know that you have some deep cover contacts that can fill you in on what I can't when they run those blood samples that you didn't think that I saw you take last night."

Tuck just grinned at Joel and replied, "I understand that your hands are tied, Joel, but I do appreciate you leveling with me about what you can't tell me. I've got a hunch anyway that probably will be confirmed tonight."

"Well, if your hunch is that this is directed at you, then you are wrong. That bunch was silenced by one of your 'friends' who sent a graphic package from the islands in response to a threat against Bob and Abigail Pike. Director Claiborne was so impressed with the effectiveness of the message; he said that if we could operate like that, we'd get a lot more accomplished, so no, the threat is not from Washington anymore," Joel told him.

"I suppose I should be relieved by that revelation, but getting killed by someone sneaking across the border is just as bad as getting killed by a lunatic from my own government. I'm still going to be dead!" Tuck told him in response to the news.

"Tuck, you have a special gift when it comes to sensing danger, and you have the acquired skills that few men have to deal with it. Between your skills and our skills, we've got this covered," Joel encouraged his friend as they pulled up at the ranch house.

"I'm going to take Hanna and Emily back to the hotel, Joel. Thanks for talking to me about this. I'll expect a full disclosure on your date tomorrow," Tuck told him with a laugh.

“You can be certain that it will be ‘fair and balanced’,” Joel laughed with him in reply, “see you guys tomorrow.”

CHAPTER 17

Tuck's burner phone rang at two o'clock the next morning, "Hello Shaun."

"Hello Tuck, I'm sorry to wake you, but the results of the samples are in. I'm sure that you didn't want to wait until morning for me to let you know what they are."

"Of course not, what have you got?" Tuck answered quietly.

"Those guys are definitely not ISIS. Both have the DNA of both Spanish and Apache Indian. What is better, one of them is in the database so we could identify him. He was Pablo Salinas the son of Isaiah Salinas who was one of the Los Zetas leaders before an FBI counter strike killed him and some of his men about twenty years ago after they kidnapped one of our female agents and demanded ransom or her death. Was there a woman with them?" Shaun finished with the question.

"No woman, just two more that we killed at the cave before the attack on the house. If these guys weren't after me, what in the world were they doing?" Tuck asked.

"They were there to kill Bradley Rumskill, the agent that killed Isaiah and five of his men after his partner died in the rescue effort," Shaun O'Brien answered.

"There's no Bradley Rumskill on that ranch! I've never heard of him," Tuck protested.

"You know him as Otis Jamieson, his witness protection identity. Apparently, there has been a leak of classified information out of the El Paso office and the Special Agent in Charge, who was also on that raid with Rumskill, has been kidnapped, and is presumed dead," Shaun gave Tuck the information that he had received.

"Tuck, you need to listen to me very closely. Pablo Salinas has a sister, Lois. Her men call her 'El Lobo Diablo', The

Devil Wolf. She is a psychopath that is every bit as brutal and well trained as he was. Her favorite weapon is a skinning knife, but she is well versed in every combat discipline. She will be coming to avenge her brother, and your family is in very grave danger," Shaun told him, "Who was it that killed Pablo anyway?"

"Hanna shot him after he shot a friend of ours in the driveway," Tuck responded.

Shaun was silent for a minute while he digested the news, then, "There is something else that you need to know. There were four men in the group that attacked the Los Zetas stronghold the night Bradley executed her father. Lois has the names of all of us now, so I am coming to Texas on the next flight out instead of waiting for her to come to me."

"You were one of them?" Tuck was amazed at the revelation, "You know Otis?"

"Keep this between us until I can get a look at the terrain. We may have to enlist some more help. Can you put me up at the ranch?" O'Brien finished.

"Of course we can Shaun. Call me when you get in and I'll pick you up at the airport," Tuck told him.

"We have a plan then; see you tomorrow," Shaun ended the call.

"I heard most of that, Michael. How bad is it going to be?" Hanna asked from the bed.

"I'm sorry Hanna; I didn't mean to wake you up. The good news is that our enemies in the government are not going to bother us again, and the not so good news is that we are going to be hunted by a Mexican cartel," Tuck tried to sound light-hearted, but came up short.

"Is that all, silly? Come back to bed and let's pray for some help and wisdom to get through this. That's what daddy would have done," Hanna replied.

Tuck crawled back in bed, and they prayed until Hanna drifted off to sleep. Tuck was still awake at daybreak, his thoughts running a gambit of scenarios against an avenging female devil.

Joel was already on his second cup of coffee when Tuck reached the dining area of the hotel just after six am.

"Good morning sunshine, what did your sources have to say last night?" Joel asked with a big cheery grin on his face.

"That's classified information, Joel. You know how that works. How was your date with Maggie last night?" Tuck returned the grin as he poured a cup of coffee from the breakfast bar.

"We had a great time, Tuck. The food was good, the atmosphere was excellent, and I had to have been with the most beautiful woman in the place the way all of the men were staring," Joel replied.

"So what time did you get in, if I might ask?" Tuck tried to sound like a protective father.

"Easy Dad, I brought the young lady back early and left her in the lobby like any gentleman would do," Joel answered with a laugh.

"I'm proud of you Mr. Biggs. Now let's talk about Los Zetas!" Tuck caught him by surprise.

"So you know. Well, that's good because you would have found out sooner or later and probably under circumstances that are more painful. I got a call from Director Claiborne this morning announcing his arrival in Midland later today. Apparently he is meeting Shaun O'Brien here, but you wouldn't know anything about that, would you?" Joel asked.

"Does Maggie know about her father coming out?" Tuck asked.

"No, and I'm not going to tell a famous newscaster anything about it. That's all we would need right now," Joel reassured him, "besides, she'll be on an airplane out of here long before he arrives...I hope."

"Good morning, boys!" Maggie strolled into the dining area where the two men were talking, "Is there anything new to report this morning...like maybe Assistant Director Claiborne flying out here today?"

"Good morning Maggie. How about those Dallas Cowboys?" Joel made a point of turning the topic to something else besides his boss visiting.

"Good morning Maggie." Tuck played the uninvolved third party to the hilt.

"I've already set up an interview with Director Claiborne at the airport when he arrives. I had to delay getting out of here, but my bosses want to know what is going on that is so important the Director is getting his boots on the ground out here," Maggie continued.

"Maggie, you can't run with that story," Joel said while reaching across the small table to place his hand on hers.

Maggie pulled her hand back as her Irish temper started to flair, "And just why can't I run with this story, Agent Biggs?"

Joel looked helplessly at Tuck who answered Maggie, "Because he's coming here to meet with your father!"

Maggie looked at the two for a minute before replying in a calmer tone, "Why?"

"All that I can tell you is this: If you report on the Director arriving here on national news, it will jeopardize all of our safety, including your father. You need to trust me on this," Joel said forcefully.

"How long do I need to sit on the story?" Maggie asked, knowing that there was something big getting ready to happen that would be a much bigger story than the travel plans of the Assistant Director of the FBI.

"Maybe a week, maybe less, plans have to be made," Joel said.

"If I stand down on this, I get the scoop on the main story, right?" Maggie threw it out there.

"Of course you do Maggie," Joel reassured her.

"One week and that is all Joel. I mean it too," Maggie replied.

"Well, at least you two are back on a first name basis," Tuck interjected with a laugh, "I've got to check on Hanna so play nice."

Noah Escobar was on his knees with his arms pulled up behind his body and blood running down his face to the dirt floor of the old building, deserted now except for the stench of the meth lab that was in full operation minutes before they dragged his unconscious body inside.

Standing in front of him was the woman that until recently he knew as Lois Freeman. Now this same woman was killing him slowly and enjoying every slice of her knife across his body while two of her men watched from the shadows, taking turns to make certain that the meth operation kept running.

"Do you remember my father now, Noah Escobar, you worthless piece of filth?" She spat the question out in Spanish as if the last four cuts had improved his memory.

Noah knew that he wouldn't last much longer at the rate that he was bleeding, but pretending ignorance to her questions had bought him a few hours more of life, and as long as there was life, there was hope.

The heat in the tin-sided building was intense, and he hadn't had a drink in more than twelve hours.

"Water, I need water," He managed to croak.

"You will need it worse when I come back with your friends," Lois said to him as she signaled to the men that were watching and left the building.

Noah heard the men leave about ten minutes after Lois Salinas. The light switch was turned off, and the tin-sheeted door of the shed was slammed shut with a chain fastened to the outside, signaling to Noah that he was alone. He rocked back on his heels to give him a little slack in the chains that held his arms, and then stood up, almost passing out from the blood loss and pain as circulation returning to his arms. He could still see out of his right eye and noticed that the chain on his right arm had a little slack in it. Working his bloody, slick hand back and forth in a twisting motion he slowly and painfully pulled his arm free of the chain. Soon the left arm followed and Noah Escobar was standing free of his chains.

He looked around in the dim light afforded by two very dirty barred windows at the methamphetamine laboratory that they had packed into the old building. The burners were fueled with several one hundred pound propane tanks and had been turned to low, which indicated that the men had probably stepped out for a beer and would be returning soon. Noah saw the hanging light fixtures with the exposed incandescent bulb and had an idea. Working as fast as his pain numbed brain and blood slick hands would allow, he unscrewed one of the low hanging bulbs close to the lab. After carefully breaking the bulb without damaging the element, he screwed it back in place, and then turned off the flame on the burners. As soon as the flame went out, Noah opened the propane tank valves so that raw propane was released into the building.

Fighting to stay conscious, Noah then moved to the back of the building and pushed against the sheet metal siding first in one spot and then another. Soon he found what he was looking for, a spot where the nails had rusted off and the siding was loose. An old two by four from a pallet was lying on the floor, and Noah used it to pry the sheet metal back far enough to wriggle out of the hole and into the bright sunlight. He found himself standing in the middle of a deserted farm in who knew where. Time was running out unless he found water and help immediately. The squeaking of an old windmill drew his attention. If there were still a few drops of water in the tank, he might revive enough to make it to freedom.

Noah staggered to the tank and looked in. In the bottom was about six inches of slime covered water and a dead rat. Staying across the tank from the rodent, Noah scooped the foul water to his mouth and satisfied his thirst. He splashed it on his head and down his back to wash off some of the blood that was oozing out of the several dozen shallow cuts that Lois had inflicted all around his aging torso.

Now he had to leave or risk being recaptured. His old Special Forces training was rusty, but still locked in his head. He headed into the desert on a northward trek after finding an old piece of canvas that he soaked in the stagnant water and draped over himself. Not only would it give him some camouflage from the air, it would also shield him from the sun, which was already sinking lower toward the western horizon.

He had gone less than a quarter of a mile when Noah felt the ground tremble at the same time as the air was split by a thunderous explosion behind him. With a smile on his bloodied face, Noah hobbled weakly on toward the Rio Grand.

CHAPTER 18

"Hanna, I've got to get back to the ranch and get ready for Brian. I think it might be best if I took you and Emily to John and Louise's...just to be safe," Tuck said to Hanna as he delivered a cup of coffee and a bagel to the room.

"Michael, I'm not going to hide from trouble. Emily and I will be going back to the ranch with you. That's our home now, and no one is going to run us off," Hanna replied to Tuck's suggestion, "Besides, I remember the 'for better or for worse' part of our vows. What kind of wife would I be if I only stuck around for the better?"

"A live one, maybe?" Tuck tried an argument that he knew would be unsuccessful.

"Don't be silly. This is going to work out in the end. You'll see. Now help me get everything packed so we can get home," Hanna said with a big smile.

Knowing that he was beaten, Tuck simply replied, "I'll go get the cart."

Joel stopped him in the lobby as he was returning to the room and took Tuck aside. "Are you going to pick Shaun O'Brien up at the airport?"

"I'm not sure. When I talked to Shaun, he just asked if he could bunk at the ranch. I'll call as soon as I get back to the room," Tuck replied, "Listen, Joel, Hanna is insisting on going back to the ranch with me today. I don't like the idea, but it is what it is. Can you get me a couple of M-4s to help with my home defense?"

"I'll do better than that, Tuck. You get Hanna situated while I meet with Director Claiborne, and I'll be in touch later this evening. Let me know about Shaun because I think the Director will probably want a very private meeting with him, and the airport won't be the place for that," Joel responded before leaving the hotel.

"Hello Tuck," Shaun O'Brien answered his call, "What's your twenty?"

"Hi Shaun, we are getting ready to go back to the ranch. The FBI is finished with their investigation, and I have work to do down there. I called to see if you needed me to pick you up at the airport?" Tuck answered.

Shaun gave him a big chuckle and then said, "I'm here at the ranch waiting for you with Director Claiborne. He thought that it might be a good ruse to let it leak that he was flying into Midland. We came in early on a Beechcraft King Air that had been confiscated in Miami. In case anyone is watching the ranch, the private markings looked like some of the other business planes in the area."

"Does Joel Biggs know? Isn't he supposed to be meeting with the Director today?" Tuck questioned.

"He does, and he is. Joel was supposed to get you to call me without arousing suspicions. Apparently, he has done an outstanding job. Now get your ass down here, we've got some plans to make," Shaun concluded. The serious nature in his tone told Tuck as much as the conversation.

"I'm on the way!" Tuck answered and ended the call.

Maggie O'Brien was leaving as Hanna and Tuck were loading the truck with the few things that they had brought from the ranch, and came over to say good-bye.

"Tuck, have you seen Joel? He was supposed to meet me here and follow us out to the airport to meet with Director Claiborne," Maggie asked after hugging Hanna and Emily.

"I think he has already left, Maggie. I saw him this morning, and he told me that he was going to pick up your father and Director Claiborne," Tuck told her an outright lie, which made Hanna turn her head and just give him 'that' look.

"Really? I'd better get going then. I think 'Agent' Biggs is trying to pull a fast one," Maggie said angrily, and then turned to get in the news van with the camera crew.

"Michael Tucker, you lied to Maggie!" Hanna said sternly.

"Yes I did, but it was for our security. They need to think that Director Claiborne is at the airport," Tuck answered in his defense.

"A lie is a lie. Michael. You should have come up with something else, something simple like you didn't know where Joel was," Hanna rebuked him.

"That would have been a lie also Hanna. Joel is on the way to the ranch," Tuck countered.

"Oh...well, you are going to have to do something for Maggie to make up for it. She'll never forgive you otherwise," Hanna replied although the force had gone out of her argument.

"Let's go feed your monkey. I'll bet the little guy is wondering what happened to us," Tuck hurriedly changed the tone of the conversation as they got into the Ford and headed back to the Thunder Ranch. While he was on the road, Tuck placed a call to the gun shop owner to check on the AK 47 serial number.

"Hello Tuck. I did have that number traced and as far as my sources can tell, that rifle left a gun shop in Tucson a few months ago with five others just like it. It would seem that they were probably part of that 'Fast and Furious' deal that recently backfired on the DOJ and gave them such a black eye," He told him.

"I'll relay that information on to the Feds down here. It will probably make Luke's day to know that he was shot with such a famous rifle," Tuck joked, "Thanks for getting this info. I'll keep you all posted on any events that I can talk about."

"Just keep your head down, Tuck. I hate to lose a good customer before he spends at least half of his money here," The owner quipped back.

Tuck laughed as he ended the call.

As he had gotten used to doing in the past few hectic months, Tuck kept a close eye on his rear view mirrors for any signs that any of the traffic behind him on 385 might be suspicious. Most of the times that he had thought that he was being followed; it was his internal alarm that clued him to possible danger. This time, as they turned off of the 338 loop unto 385, Tuck looked back and saw the local Fox affiliate news van making the same turn just a few cars back.

"Well, Hanna, it looks like old Maggie didn't believe the story that I gave her about Joel going to the airport," He told Hanna while motioning with his thumb behind them.

"Michael, you shouldn't have gotten her upset with Joel. Now she's going to mess up the plans that those men are making, and she might get into trouble," Hanna replied.

"Let me call Joel and see if he can do something about this," Tuck said to her as he reached for his phone.

"Hello Tuck, are you on the way?" Joel answered.

"Yeah, we're rolling, but your girlfriend is too, and I don't think she is too happy with you," Tuck answered.

"What do you mean? I thought that you were going to tell her that I was at the airport?" Joel sounded alarmed.

"I just turned on 385, and she's about six cars back in the news van with her camera crew. What's the plan?" Tuck reported.

"There's a team set up at the first gate. When you pass through, they will close the road to all traffic that is behind you. Maggie probably won't speak to me again, but she can't be allowed to run with this story just yet. By the way, can you stop at that Stripes in McCamey and pick up six hamburgers? The director is starving," Joel replied.

Tuck just shook his head as he responded to Joel's request, "I'm not going to stop with that angry red head behind me. You'll have to send out for them."

"I'll call you right back," Joel said as he ended the call.

"What did he say?" Hanna asked.

"He wanted me to stop in McCamey for hamburgers for the director...like that is going to happen," Tuck replied.

"Michael, I can handle Maggie. You go ahead and stop," Hanna told him, "Besides, I'd like one too, and I don't want to cook when we get there."

Tuck just nodded and kept looking in the mirror. About ten minutes later, a DPS trooper was heading in the opposite direction at high speed and did a u-turn across traffic, pulling up behind the news van with his lights on.

"Boy, Joel has really dug his grave with Maggie now!" Tuck exclaimed while looking in his rear view mirror at the news van pulling over to the side of the road.

Before Hanna could respond, his phone rang, "Now about those burgers..," Joel said laughing.

"We were going to stop anyway. You know that this probably means that Hanna and I won't be attending your wedding anytime soon," Tuck told his friend, "Ask the Director what he wants on his burgers."

"Mustard on all of them," Joel laughed and hung up.

"No onions on mine Michael, they will get right into my milk and might upset Emily," Hanna said with a smile.

Even though they beat the oil field lunch crowd, the stop at the Stripes seemed to take forever, and Tuck kept looking out of the station window for any sign of Maggie and the news crew, but didn't see them. They were soon back on the highway headed for the ranch when Tuck checked the rear view and there was the van, three cars back and holding its position.

When they reached I-10 for the short run to the next exit and the road to the ranch, Maggie's crew shot past the Ford in a determined effort to reach the ranch and Maggie's story of a lifetime.

Tuck stayed under the eighty mile per hour posted speed limit and arrived at the ranch gate just in time to see two county sheriff's deputies in full SWAT gear stop the van and order all of the occupants out. Two more Deputies motioned Tuck and Hanna through the gate while Maggie O'Brien glared at the Ford as it passed by. Tuck kept his gaze straight ahead, but Hanna smiled and gave a small wave to the now furious red headed news lady.

"Here is what we know so far," Director John Claiborne told the men assembled at the table after the introductions were made, "Late yesterday, there was a large explosion south west of Juarez about fifteen miles in a largely deserted area. Mexican authorities have investigated what they are telling us is an old farm building that was being used as a drug processing site for a Los Zetas group. They also found a badly burned survivor that has confirmed, and I expect under their special type of methods, that Noah Escobar was being held there by Lois Salinas. Since his body was not in the rubble, there is a very slim chance that he is alive.

The authorities are searching between where the explosion occurred here and Guadalupe for Special Agent Escobar and you can bet the Lois Salinas has a better equipped group searching the same area," Director Claiborne finished using a map that had been rolled out on the table for reference.

The meeting was interrupted by a single-engine aircraft buzzing low over the roof of the house and continuing on to the airstrip. The men hurriedly loaded into one of the SUVs and drove to the airstrip to meet the unexpected guest. They arrived as the Cessna Caravan taxied to the east end of the airstrip and parked next to the Beechcraft. The security detail that followed Director Claiborne, Shaun O'Brien, Joel, and Tuck to the airstrip trained their M-4s on the plane as they waited for the passengers to disembark, and they weren't kept in suspense. Otis Jamieson, aka Bradley Rumskill climbed out of the airplane with a big wave.

John Claiborne and Shaun O'Brien walked toward the plane to meet their old running mate, while Tuck and Joel waited by the vehicle. When the men came back Otis/Bradley walked up to Tuck and shook his hand, "Tuck, I'm sorry that this trouble has come on you and your wife. The Lord knows that you've had enough to last you both a lifetime. I left Julia with Henry Albright up in Washington State, and this plane is waiting to take Mrs. Tucker and the baby to them until this crisis is resolved."

"Hanna won't go, Otis. She can be a very determined woman," Tuck responded.

"Make no mistake about this Tuck. If Hanna stays, it is very likely that Lois Salinas will kill her and your baby, and probably you too. If she goes, she's safe no matter what happens down here in the next day or two," Otis told him sternly.

"I'll talk to her when we go back," Tuck responded. He knew that Otis was right, but convincing Hanna to go would be difficult.

"It might not be that hard, Tuck. I talked to Henry right before we landed, and he was going to have a discussion with your wife," Otis said with a smile, "Relax Tuck, that uncle of hers is probably more capable than we are of protecting her."

That seemed like an odd statement for Otis to make, but Tuck let it pass.

They loaded back into the vehicles, the pilot of the Cessna getting into the security team's SUV, and returned to the ranch house where Hanna was waiting outside for Tuck.

"Michael, I just got off of the phone with Uncle Henry. He explained why I need to take Emily out of here," Hanna spoke with tears in her eyes.

"Hanna, we are going to be okay. If you are with Henry then I know that you are safe too. Otis is waiting on an answer," Tuck told her as he held her close.

"I'll have our stuff ready in about thirty minutes Michael. Are you sure you'll be alright?" She asked quietly.

"Absolutely sure Hon, absolutely sure" Tuck answered.

Forty-five minutes later, Tuck held back a tear as the Cessna climbed over the mesquite covered bluffs and headed toward safety for his wife and daughter.

CHAPTER 19

The sound of traffic brought Noah Escobar out of his stupor in the dark of night, and he realized that he must have passed out. About one hundred yards in the front of him was a four-lane highway, Mexico 45. He managed to slowly stand and start moving towards the highway in hopes of flagging down a passing motorist, although in this area, they would quite likely be either farmers or cartel members. As he got closer to the main road, Noah saw several vehicles standing on the road shoulder nearest to him and decided to risk all or nothing in an attempt to get help. As he approached the lead car, he noticed that it was marked with the emblem of the Mexican Police, which might or might not be a good thing since many were taking bribes from the more powerful of the cartels.

One of the men turned to look off into the desert and spotted him standing about twenty-five feet from the car. Noah's last reserves had given out, and he sunk to the ground as the young officer shouted to his men before running over to look at the bloodied man that was on his knees with his head bowed. Within fifteen minutes, a rescue helicopter was on the scene, and Noah Escobar was whisked away for emergency medical attention and a meeting with his old teammates.

"Gentlemen, we have confirmation that Noah Escobar is in route to Fort Bliss. Shaun and I will be leaving immediately to debrief him. We believe that this may be our best chance to get one-step ahead of Lois Salinas and whatever else she might have planned. Brad will be in charge of security and our operations here. Joel and Tuck, you two will set up a forward security station where you can watch the airfield and the ranch house. No air traffic will be permitted until we return. There are two FIM-92 Stinger missiles in the back of the Yukon, and you are authorized to use them against any aircraft that displays hostile intent or tries to land here in our absence. Is that understood?" John Claiborne briefed the men.

"Yes sir," Otis answered for everyone at the table, "I'll get started on security by checking with the men that are stationed along the main road coming in. Tuck, you take Joel to the west end of the bluff that runs parallel to the airstrip. It's rough getting to it, but the Yukon should be able to take you most of the way. The outcroppings will provide cover from overhead, and the location is high enough that you can see the runway from the west end."

"I know the spot, and I think that we can get that Yukon in there," Tuck answered.

The said their goodbyes to Shaun and Director Claiborne and drove past the furthest end of the runway and down into the dry gully that ran below the base of the bluff that Otis had picked to set up the forward security outpost. Tuck pulled into the heavy mesquite and maneuvered the Yukon along the dry bed until they reached a point about four hundred feet below the outcropping.

"Well, this should hide the vehicle well enough. It looks like a hump to the top for us though," He said to Joel, who seemed distracted, "Joel, is everything all right?"

"Everything is fine Tuck. Let's get set up," Joel answered.

They got out to unload the vehicle, and as Tuck was reaching for his gear, he heard Joel behind him.

"Okay Tuck, lets see your hands on the top of your head," Joel told him in no uncertain terms.

"What's going on Joel?" Tuck asked as he complied with Joel's demand.

Joel pulled Tuck's hands behind him and used two zip ties to secure them together behind his back, "You can turn around now."

Tuck turned to see the Beretta in Joel's hand pointing directly at his face, "Have you lost your mind? What in the hell is going on?"

"Settle down Tuck. It is all about economics. Lois Salinas is paying one hundred grand in cash for each one of you that I kill, and a bonus, so I figure that a half a million in cash talks to me a little stronger than our short friendship. Now, I have to get that Stinger out of the truck before the Director gets airborne, and then I'll come back to deal with you," Joel told him as he dragged the case with the surface to air missile out of the back of the SUV, "Now sit down against that hitch ball."

Joel zip tied Tuck's neck to the hitch ball so that he couldn't move without choking, and then went up along the face of the bluff with the missile pack. Tuck knew there was nothing he could do to stop Joel from shooting down the turbo prop when it departed in the next few minutes, and very probably couldn't do anything to prevent his demise at Joel's hands shortly afterward. He remembered watching George Withers trying in vain to get free of the mast trunk on the Night Wind.

The minutes seemed to drag by for an eternity, and then the sound of the Beechcraft revving up for a takeoff reached Tuck's ears. Shortly after that, a blood-curdling scream ripped through the air followed by the explosion of the S.A.M. as it impacted the bottom of the steep slope several hundred feet below where Joel had fired it.

Tuck struggled to turn his head in the direction of the scream, but his vision was held straight down the gully where they had just parked. He sat there for several minutes wondering if anyone would think to check on the explosion, when a movement fifty feet behind the SUV caught his attention. Looking up at him as it stepped out of the mesquite cover was the badly burned and enraged black panther that had just attacked Joel and was now looking for another victim.

It took two slow steps toward Tuck and crouched to attack when the cat was knocked off of its feet in a spray of red followed by the crack of a large caliber rifle. Tuck then heard a Polaris engine running wide open as one of the ATVs tore up the dry streambed. Otis slid the Ranger around the corner and past the dead cat at full speed until he saw Tuck sitting behind the Yukon.

Skidding to a stop, Otis jumped out and ran to get Tuck cut loose, "Are you all right, Tuck? Where's Joel?"

"Joel is working for them, I guess. I'm fine, but I think we need to check on him. That cat did something that caused the missile to fire downhill," Tuck said calmly as he got up and went to the rear seat of the car to retrieve his Kimber and the .308.

The two men hurriedly climbed to the area where the panther had recently established a new den, and there was Joel, lying with his back severely burned from firing the missile prone, and his head badly mauled with a portion of the skull missing. Tuck knelt beside him and checked his vitals before turning to Otis and giving a negative shake of his head, signifying that Joel wasn't long for this life.

"Who were you working for, Joel?" Otis asked him as the breathing became shallower.

"Freelance!" Joel exclaimed in a very weak voice, "Lois Salinas has a bounty on you that made my salary look like peanuts, even more on these others. I could have been rich."

"Well son, where you're going you could have spent it on ice. Good luck with that now," Otis told him.

"Joel, I wish that it was different, but you aren't going to make it back off of this hill," Tuck said to him, "Is there any message that you want me to carry?"

"Right now I'm sorry about a lot of things, Tuck, but I'm kind of glad that panther got me before I killed you," He looked at Tuck and then in a very weak whisper said, "She knows...," Joel eyes grew dull and the death rattle sounded in his throat.

"Who does? She knows what, Joel?" He asked, but his ex-friend was gone.

"Did the Director and Shaun take off?" Tuck asked Otis after closing Joel's eyes.

"No they've aborted the flight until I report in. Let's get back down to the airstrip and brief them about this," Otis replied looking at Joel's body.

"What about him?" Tuck asked pointing toward Joel.

"He's in Hell, nothing can help him now," Otis said as he walked away.

"I'm concerned about the last words that he spoke. Who do you think that he was referring to?" Tuck asked Otis.

"I'm guessing it would have to be Lois Salinas. What she knows is anybody's guess though," Otis replied as they made their way back down the hill.

"Who would have thought that Agent Joel Biggs would sellout as a mercenary to a drug cartel?" John Claiborne asked, "This whole operation is turning into a nightmare, and it's all because one of our senor agents couldn't control his lust for young women. Now we have lost a brilliant young agent and all of the information that he had pertaining to that same operation is in the hands of a psychopathic killer. What were his last words again, Tuck?"

"He said 'She knows...' and nothing after that," Tuck answered.

"Well, we have to assume that she knows everything about our plans, including the fact that your wife is on the way to

Henry Albright's in Washington State. Tuck, you need to make a call to Henry immediately and tell him about this development. The rest of us need to come up with another plan of attack to level the playing field," Shaun O'Brien spoke up.

"Tuck, make your call to Henry and then pack your gear, all of us are going to El Paso," Director Claiborne added, "That goes for you too Brad, I think that we need your special touch to finish this business as quickly as possible."

While the men made calls to various agencies for Intel and support, Tuck called Henry Albright.

"Hello Tuck, Hanna isn't here yet. Do you want her to call you when she gets in?" Henry answered his phone.

"Henry, Hanna's cover is blown, and the sister of the man she shot knows that she is coming to you," Tuck blurted out.

"Well, that's a bitch, Tuck, but I can handle it from here. Tell them not to radio the plane with any other instructions, and I'll take care of everything when it lands. Now you just get your job done down there and don't worry about Hanna. Everything is under control," Henry reassured him.

"Thanks Henry. I've got to get back into the meeting. I'll call when it is over," Tuck ended the call.

Tuck walked back into the room and relayed to Shaun what Henry had told him about radioing the airplane that was carrying Hanna and Emily.

"That makes sense Tuck, especially if they are monitoring the radio frequency that we are using. Henry shows good sense, and I think that we need to put all of our energy into stopping Lois Salinas," Shaun replied, "We will need your rifle packed with your gear, Tuck. You've been drafted again."

CHAPTER 20

"Mrs. Tucker?" the pilot of the Cessna Caravan called back to Hanna who was two seats behind him taking care of Emily.

"Yes?" She answered.

"I am going to land for fuel at the Sierra Blanca Airport in about twenty minutes. There is a small pilot's lounge that you can use while you wait," The pilot told her.

"Why can't I wait with the plane?" Hanna asked.

"It's against regulations, Ma'am. Everybody has to disembark while I am fueling. Don't worry. It won't take long, and then we will be non-stop to Washington," He answered.

Hanna tried to read his facial expression, but couldn't see much from behind. Besides, he was wearing aviator glasses that hid his eyes. She tried to think of what Tuck would do or say in this situation, and she was sure that he would be suspicious of anything that triggered his 'gut instinct' as hers was being triggered now. She reached quietly for the phone and sent Tuck a text, "Landing in Sierra Blanca for fuel. Check it out."

The plane landed and taxied to a small maintenance building just off of the east end of the paddock and close to the highway. When it came to a stop, the pilot helped her and Emily off the plane while he arranged for fuel. Hanna walked across the apron and entered the small break area; immediately turning around and watching the pilot who was standing next to the Cessna and talking on the cell phone while gesturing at the door that she had just gone through.

Her phone buzzed indicating an incoming text from Tuck. It read, "Get out of there. Get out of there now! I am on the way."

Hanna didn't stop when she reached the small lobby area; instead, she walked directly across the building and out of the back door into a parking area just off of Highway 220.

"Please God protect my child. We really need your help right now," She prayed as she walked across the parking lot to the road. Just as she arrived at the edge of the highway a Lincoln County Sheriff's deputy drove up and slowed down to look at the woman with an infant standing with a bewildered look on the side of the road.

"Ma'am, are you alright?" he asked when he rolled down the window of his Toyota Tundra pickup.

"I need help!" Hanna blurted out, "Can you take me somewhere safe?"

"Yes Ma'am. I can take you to the Sheriff's office over in Carrizozo. I'm headed in right now myself. Come on and get in," The deputy replied.

Hanna raced to the other side of the truck and got in the back with Emily

"Please hurry, these people won't care if you are a deputy or not if they see me in this truck. We are both in danger," She pleaded as she saw the pilot walk out of the building's rear entrance and look around for her.

As the Deputy drove off toward Carrizozo, Hanna shared her story with him. It was soon obvious that he wasn't buying the urgency of the situation that she was trying to convey. As they neared the top of a group of mountains, Hanna checked her phone signal and dialed Tuck.

"Hanna! Are you okay? What's going on?' Tuck's voice was uncharacteristically tinged with anxiety.

"Michael, I haven't got time to talk right now, but I need for you to explain to this deputy sheriff how dangerous my situation is," Hanna handed the phone to the surprised deputy.

"This is Deputy Burgess speaking," He answered, "Yes sir, yes sir. I understand sir. I'll tell the sheriff as soon as we get in. Yes sir, I can give you his phone number. It's 575-555-1212. Here she is."

Hanna took the phone back from the shaking hand of the deputy who immediately sped up to eighty miles an hour and turned his lights on, "Michael? What in the world did you say?"

"This is John Claiborne, Mrs. Tucker. Here's your husband," Director Claiborne answered.

"Hanna everything is going to be all right. The director is calling the Sheriff up there and making arrangements for your and Emily's safety until I can get to you," Tuck told her.

"Michael, what happened? How did they find Emily and me?" Hanna asked.

"Joel sold us out, Hon. I couldn't believe it, but it happened," Tuck said quietly.

"Joel? I can't believe it. Where is he now?" Hanna asked in shock.

"Well, based on everything that I believe, he's in Hell!" Tuck exclaimed.

"Oh no Michael, you didn't kill him did you?" Hanna was mortified at the thought.

"No, he died by the hand of God. That's the only way to explain what happened and the timing of it," Tuck explained.

"Michael, I'm losing the signal. I'll call as soon as we are safe," Hanna finished just as the broken signal beep sounded in her ear.

"Deputy Burgess, how much further to the Sheriff's office?" she asked sweetly.

"Mrs. Tucker, I've called the sheriff, and he is coming with an armed escort to take us the rest of the way in. We'll probably meet them in about five miles," The deputy answered. It was apparent that he had the crap scared out of him and just wanted to be out of that vehicle that was now a target for one of the most deadly gangs in Mexico and the Border States.

Just as Deputy Burgess told her, the Sheriff of Lincoln County New Mexico was waiting with three other vehicles when the deputy sped by. They quickly took up positions in the front and the rear of the Deputy's Tundra, and Hanna could see at least two men in each truck besides the driver. She should have felt relief with this number of law enforcement personnel concentrating on her safety, but Hanna knew that there was going to be no peace of mind until the word came that Lois Salinas was dead.

The convoy soon arrived at the Sheriff's office and the men formed a protective corridor for Hanna and the baby before they would let her out of the truck. Once inside, she was ushered into a back room and into the presence of Sheriff Roy Blackman, a large man with black hair, graying at the temples and a smile as large as Texas.

"Mrs. Tucker, I'm Sheriff Roy Blackman, but you can call me Roy," He said as he introduced himself, "These men are my deputies until this crisis is over with."

Sheriff Roy gestured around the room at the steely-eyed, weather beaten bunch of men that seemed to have stepped out of an old western movie.

"Thank you for taking care of us, Sheriff Roy. I assume that you've already been briefed about what is going on?" Hanna asked.

"Yes ma'am, I talked to Director Claiborne while you were on the way here, and he filled me in on what is at stake. You can bet that we're not going to let anything happen to you or your baby," Sheriff Roy assured her, "I've got a ranch out away from here that has an airstrip on it. We are going to move you out there and wait for the Calvary to arrive."

Hanna just smiled at him and said, "Thank you Sheriff, and thank all of you men too. Can I have a private spot to nurse Emily before we go?"

"Absolutely, Ma'am, just follow Deputy Alice over there, and she will sit with you until you're ready to leave," Sheriff Roy indicated a tall rawboned lady deputy with a big smile on her sun burned face.

Hanna left the room feeling relaxed for the first time since that morning and realized that the anxiety caused by her gut instinct alarm had died down.

Once the plane carrying Director Claiborne, Shaun O'Brien, Otis, and Tuck arrived in El Paso, it was hurriedly refueled for a trip to Sheriff Blackman's ranch near Ruidoso to pick up Hanna and deliver her to Henry Albright in Newport, Washington near the Idaho border. Otis and Tuck would make that trip while John Claiborne and Shaun debriefed Noah Escobar to glean whatever they could from him that would help track down Lois Salinas, it was a matter of hunting the hunter, and the one that solved this deadly game of 'cat and mouse' first would live.

Claiborne had called in military help in stopping the Cessna and its pilot from escaping into Mexico, and the men waited for an update from the F-16 pilots that had intercepted the plane before it left New Mexico airspace.

"Sir, do we have permission to fire on this airplane?" Claiborne was asked.

"Not unless they won't land before leaving our airspace. If that doesn't seem to be likely to happen, terminate that flight with extreme prejudice," He ordered.

Now all they could do was wait. It was hoped that the pilot could be captured because he probably had information that would help them understand Lois' plans, but if he couldn't be caught, then dead was the next best thing.

After ten minutes of waiting, a call came that verified the termination of the Cessna and its pilot over an unpopulated area of desert in southern New Mexico. Director Claiborne scrambled a team to the site of the crash to glean whatever evidence might be found, and Tuck's flight barreled off into the night to pick up Hanna and Emily. Little did they know that the hunt for Lois Salinas was taking place eleven hundred miles south of where she was plotting her revenge.

CHAPTER 21

Maggie O'Brien tried Joel Biggs' phone for the third or fourth time that day without success. She had left two voice mails that remained unanswered, and her news director was pressuring her for a story based on the information that they had received about the Assistant Director of the FBI flying to Midland, Texas. Angry at the fact that Joel and Tuck had both misled her, she turned to the one person that she knew would at least tell her the truth, Shaun O'Brien.

Shaun had just stepped out of the hospital room where Noah Escobar was being treated for his injuries and loss of blood when his phone buzzed.

"O'Brien here," he answered curtly without looking at the caller I.D.

"Daddy, it's me, Maggie. I need to talk to you. Have you got a second?" Maggie felt like a little girl again, whenever she talked to the father that she never really knew, but thought of him as seven feet tall.

Shaun hesitated briefly, dreading what was coming next, "Sure Maggie, what can I do?"

"Can you tell me where Joel is? I've been trying to reach him all day, but he hasn't returned my phone calls or messages. I know that he can be a jerk, but this is not like him," Maggie blurted out to her father, forgetting her anger with Joel and replacing it with genuine concern.

"Maggie, I've got some bad news for you, and I wish that I could be there to give it to you in person, but Joel is dead. He was killed today at the ranch in an accident," Shaun told her the bad news, omitting the part where Joel had turned traitor, by agreement with the other members of the team.

"Joel...is...dead?" she asked slowly.

"I'm afraid so Maggie. The FBI will be sending his body back to his family in Myrtle Beach. Listen, I need you to sit on this news until the family can be notified. Can you do that for me?" He asked.

Maggie O'Brien, the professional reporter, came to the surface, "Of course I can, but I am under a lot of pressure from my boss to come up with the story that was supposed to be told when you and Director Claiborne flew out here. What can you give me?"

"As you already know, the Tuckers were attacked on the Thunder Ranch by ISIS terrorists. We have called together a task force to root out other cells that are operating in the border areas of Texas. That's why we are here in El Paso, to build a joint task force with the Border Patrol for that purpose. I'll make a couple of calls tonight and have one of our spokespersons contact you tomorrow with the details. You will have an exclusive on this story, so run with it," Shaun lied to his daughter to cover what they were really doing in El Paso.

"Thanks Daddy. I love you," Maggie said in a small voice.

"I love you too, and I am proud of you, Maggie," Shaun ended the call.

Maggie stared at her phone screen for a minute before the tears started rolling unchecked down her cheeks. She had felt something special when she was with Joel Biggs, and now he was dead. Tomorrow she had to catch a flight back to New York, but tonight she was going to get drunk!

"John, I just told my daughter about Biggs without letting her know about his activities. We really need to throw her a bone soon, like tomorrow morning," O'Brien said to John Claiborne when the latter stepped out of Noah's room.

"I'll handle it tonight Shaun. I'm certain that we have someone in Washington that can make up a story about an averted ISIS threat down here. The President isn't going to like that, but just between us, I'm pretty fed up with the crap that we've been taking from that office. Besides, we know that they are in here because our Border Patrol has spotted their gear. Maybe they'll keep their heads down if they think that we are on to them," Director Claiborne said in agreement, "By the way, I'm retiring Noah effective immediately. His extracurricular activities have caused us a lot of trouble, and hurt the morale of the troops in the office here. There may well be prison time for him also. You met Agent Grooms today. What do you think of him as a replacement?" Claiborne asked.

"He seems to be capable enough to take over, but having only shaken his hand; I can't really tell you if he is the man or not," Shaun replied, "What's our next step in finding Lois Salinas and her gang?"

"Well, we don't know how much damage that Biggs did to our plans. Those last words of his were vague. Right now, I think we wait for Brad and Tuck to get back, and then one of us will have to act as bait...unless you have another plan, of course," He ended with a smile.

"I'm going to call in a few favors tonight. I haven't been away from here quite as long as you have. Who knows, I might get lucky and turn something up," Shaun told him.

Knowing O'Brien's skill set, John Claiborne cautioned him, "Shaun, good hunting, but don't leave a trail tonight. I'll see you in the morning unless something comes up."

"You worry too much. That little exercise in Washington last week was just to get that clown's attention. He'll be back on solid food in a week or two, so no harm done," Shaun shook his hand and answered him with a laugh before leaving the hospital.

O'Brien hailed a cab and had it drop him at one of his old haunts in Juarez. In the dark and smoky bar, he quickly made out at least three men with an arrogant military air on the pool tables that could have the information that he was seeking, and made his way over to them.

"Hola Grandpa," One of the men said sarcastically to the laughter of them all.

O'Brien just smiled and laid his money on the table rail for the next game.

The tallest and ugliest of the three turned to the others and said laughing, "Voy a tomar el dinero de este viejo tonto, y luego una patada en su culo!"

Shaun stood there for a minute smiling while his hand searched for the right grip on his wooden cue, "My ugly Amigo, I am not anybody's fool, and I seriously doubt that you can either take my money or kick my ass."

One of the men ran around the table to get behind him, while the ugly one came at him head on. Shaun immediately reached up and snapped the end off of the cue leaving a long sharp skewer which he stuck deep into the ugly man's stomach with a lightning fast jab. He released the quivering que immediately and spun to face his next attacker. Grabbing a ball off of the table he threw it into the face of the attacker behind him and followed it with a kick to the throat as the man's head snapped back.

Turning to the third man who had not moved, he said, "I need some information pronto or you will be joining your friends."

"Senor I am just a simple man. I have no information that would help you," The man said as he sat the pool que against the table, and then moved his right hand slowly behind his back.

Shaun pulled the que from the stomach of the moaning fellow on the floor and stepped across him toward the other one.

"If your hand comes out from behind your back with anything but fingers on it, I am going to kill you," He growled.

The hand started slowly back and Shaun could see the pearl handle of a razor in it. He threw the que under hand like a javelin straight at the man's throat where it buried itself deeply just below the jaw and severed the Cartoid artery. The whole bar now in shock as they watched this gringo devastate the men that they thought were the toughest hombres in Juarez. The bartender, an older skinny Hispanic woman with dyed red hair and a high mileage look, came around the corner of the bar toward Shaun.

"These men are Los Zetas, Senor. I think that you need to leave before the rest come to kill you."

Shaun took a fifty dollar bill from his pocket and gave it to her, "My apologies for the mess, but I only wanted some information from them."

Now suddenly his best friend, the woman asked, "What type of information do you need? Is it worth anything to you?"

Shaun grinned as he realized that the bartender must have overheard anything that was said by these men as she poured the drinks.

"I'm looking for Lois Salinas," He said simply and pulled another fifty form his pocket.

"I am afraid that you are looking in the wrong place, Senor," The bartender said with a laugh as she reached for the other fifty dollars, "She is in Washington State."

"Shaun pulled the money back out of reach and asked, "Where did you hear this? How long ago?"

"Those hombres were laughing about how she was going to Washington to kill some gringo woman. That's all that I know," She replied as her hand came out expectantly.

Shaun handed her the bill with a smile, "Gracias, mucho gracias."

Shortly after he left the bar, he heard the police in route and cut through some alleys before getting back to an area where he could hail a cab like any other tourist. As he got into the cab, he made a call to John Claiborne.

"John, Lois Salinas is already in Washington! I just got the information five minutes ago. She's up there to kill Hanna, which means that Julia and Henry are in jepordy also!" he exclaimed, "I'll be back in about thirty minutes if you can call the bridge and fast track me."

"I'll make the calls immediately. Hurry up and get back here, I'm going to send you up with our spec ops team," John Claiborne replied to the bad news.

Brad and Tuck landed on the small dirt runway at Sheriff Roy Blackman's ranch just before dark and were immediately ushered to the ranch house that was surrounded with armed deputies.

"Come in Mr. Tucker!" Sheriff Blackman met them at the door.

"Thanks for taking care of my wife Sheriff. I owe you," Tuck answered as Hanna came running up to him, "This is Brad Rumskill with the El Paso office of the FBI. He's escorting us to Priest River."

"Good to meet you Brad," The sheriff said as he shook his hand, "I've sent my deputies to fuel up the Beechcraft so you can get on out of here so while your waiting, let's have a bite to eat."

Tuck was just starting to follow them into the dining room when his phone rang, "Hello, Tucker here."

"Tuck is Brad close by?" Shaun asked.

"He's right in front of me. We just got here and are going to grab a bite before we head out," Tuck answered, his instincts telling him that something was amiss.

"Lois Salinas is somewhere near where Henry and Julia are in Newport. They are in danger, and Brad needs to know. We've notified our people there, and I'm on my way with an ops team, but we'll be hours behind you. Do you understand?" Shaun stressed the urgency to Tuck.

"I think I've got the picture, Shaun. You want us to kill Lois Salinas before she kills us. Well, that was kind of my plan also. We're on it. I'll call as soon as we're wheels up," Tuck ended the call and looked up to see everyone staring at him.

"Brad, Lois beat us there. She's somewhere close to Henry and Julia, and Shaun wants us to kill her. You feeling up to it?" He asked.

Brad was heading for the door before Tuck finished so he and Hanna said good-byes all around and followed him out with Emily. Tuck turned before walking out and asked Sheriff Blackman, "Do you have a couple of M-4s that we could borrow and a few mags?"

"Of course Mr. Tucker, I'll just put them on the fuel tab. Good luck and happy hunting," He responded while motioning for two of his men to give them their weapons and vests.

"Thanks Sheriff. We'll keep you posted on how things turn out," Tuck told him as he turned to get in the SUV for the ride to the airplane.

"Get me some good publicity, this is an election year," Sheriff Roy laughed.

CHAPTER 22

"Audrey, it's been three hours since Brad called, so they should be getting into the Priest River airport in about thirty minutes. I've got to run over there and pick them up, and you should probably come with me, just in case," Henry said to Brad's wife.

"I'll be fine here until you get back Henry. There has not even been a car on that road down there in over an hour. Leave me a gun just in case and go on so you can get them back here," Audrey Rumskill replied.

"There's a shotgun behind every door. Keep the lights off and the doors bolted after I leave, and call one of us if anything is out of the ordinary. Now listen, we've got a pack of Canadian grays that run up here along the lake. These things will go one fifty to two hundred pounds, and they don't much care what they eat, so do not go outside for any reason," Henry told her.

He left the house and got into his old Jeep Wagoner. The Jeep was a gas hog, but the 390 V-8 had enough power to push a plow when the snow got deep. Thirty minutes later he pulled up to the baggage area just in time to meet Tuck, Brad, Hanna and Emily, and two FBI agents coming out.

"I don't have a chld seat Hanna. Do you think bringing Emily to a gun fight is a good idea?" Henry looked worried.

"Don't worry Uncle Henry. I'm not planning on getting shot at tonight, and Emily will be just fine, her Daddy is here," Hanna reassured him.

Tuck just looked at her and hoped he was up to the task as he handed an M-4 and a vest to Brad who was riding shotgun. Henry was running the old jeep hard with the FBI agents behind him as they made the run back through Newport and up to the cabin on Marshall Lake. As they navigated the narrow winding dirt path that meandered around the lake, Harry suddenly stopped and looked up the hill above the road at the cabin.

"The porch light is on, something's wrong," He said, "We'll need to go up on foot just in case someone is plannning a surprise party. Hanna, I want you to take the car down the road about one hundred yards to where it starts to turn to the right. Wait for us there. If we're not back in a few minutes, get the hell out of here and go for help."

"We're going to be fine, do like Henry says," Tuck told her as he got quietly out of the car. He walked back to the FBI agents and asked one of them to stay in the jeep with Hanna.

Henry led the climb up through the pitch black woods until they could see the cabin. He signalled Tuck to follow him in, and Brad went around back with the FBI agent.

Hanna coasted the old jeep quietly down the hill with the lights off to the spot where Henry had told her to park, and waited. Down by the lake she heard the eerie sound of a large wolf pack running and thought of all the trouble that the out of control re-introduction program had caused her and her family. She had placed Emily in the back seat with the seat belt around her and her blanket and was just about to get out and check on her when the sound of gunfire erupted from the cabin. At the same time, a car that was parked about fifty yards further down the road and facing her turned on its lights. Before Hanna had time to think, the FBI agent jumped out and started to advance on the other vehicle with his pistol drawn when he was cut down by a hail of bullets from an automatic rifle.

Hanna, following pure instinct, reached the ignition and started the jeep, simultaneously turning on the blinding plow lights by accident. Yanking the shift lever down into low, she floored the heavy Jeep and felt the powerful engine throw it forward like it had been loosed from a catapult. The automatic rifle opened up behind the car just as she ducked behind the dash, and a rain of broken glass fell all around her. There was no place for the driver of the small import to manuever and the heavy metal bracket that held the snow plow in the winter season drove deep into the left front fender of the car, throwing it up against a large pine and crushing the shooter between them.

Hanna slammed violently against the steering wheel but was able to put the jeep in reverse and back off of the car just as Lois Slainas tried to get out of the opposite door.

"Your not getting away, bitch!" Hanna shouted and threw the jeep back down into the car again, knocking it down the side of the mountain towards the lake.

The engine on the jeep stalled on the second impact, and Hanna sat amidst the broken glass from the shattered windows while listening to the crashing of the car as it slid down through the trees, carrying the hapless Lois Salinas along with it.

As the car carrying Lois smashed its way down the steep slope of the mountain through the sparse vegetation that grew beneath the heavy forest canopy, it rolled twice and came to a rest on its top about fifty yards from the lake shore.

Dazed and bruised from being thrown around in the tumbling car, she pulled herself slowly out of the passenger side window opening which was now barely large enough for her slight body to get through. Lois struggled to stand outside of the wreckage and looked back up the two hundred feet that her car had slid, to the lights of the Jeep that Hanna Albright was sitting in.

Reaching for the razor sharp skinning knife that she always carried in a holster that hung between her shoulder blades,

Lois was starting the climb back to wreak her vengeance on the woman that killed her brother when she heard the pack of wolves in full voice as they rushed to investigate the sound of the crash. She turned slowly to face this new danger just as the alpha male, a two hundred pounder that looked larger with his black winter fur standing up, rounded the end of the car with his female and ten other pack members.

Lois held the knife in front of her as she tried to back up the steep grade away from the pack of monsters in front of her, but several of the pack worked quickly to encircle her and prevent her escape. Knowing that she had no chance left to survive, Lois hurled herself directly at the large alpha with a savage scream and managed one clean stroke with the knife as the surprised animal turned away from the unexpected assault.

Her victory was short lived however, as the alpha female rushed in and tore at Lois' throat which she tried to shield with her left arm. As Lois raised her right arm to stab the female, another member of the pack grabbed at her wrist. Suddenly several of the animals including the bleeding leader, had sunk their fangs into various parts of her body and proceeded to rip the life from her in a vicious attack. Her screams of terror and pain did nothing to stop the assault, and the wolves slowly tore her into pieces.

Hanna heard the screams of a human being in agony and terror as the pack began to feed, and sat for a second before climbing over the seat to check on Emily who was sound asleep, protected from the impact and broken glass by the thick layers of blanket that her mother had bundled her in.

After retreiving the rifle from the back seat, she then crawled back into the front seat and started the jeep again, "Let's go check on your daddy, sweety," She said as she backed up the hill to the drive for the cabin. Holding the M-4 across her lap, Hanna drove right up to the front just as Tuck came running out followed by Henry holding his arm.

Henry had unscrewed the light bulb on the porch as soon as he got to it, and then went in the front door with Tuck behind him carrying the Kimber cocked and the safety off. Just as they entered the darkened living room a shadowy figure got behind Henry and stuck a long bladed butcher knife not so gently against his throat.

"Tell your friend to drop his gun or I will slit your throat," The man said in a thick Hispanic accent.

"Did you get that, Tuck? I think he means business," Henry gasped.

Tuck quickly raised the Kimber and fired one shot directly into Henry's upper left arm. The 240 grain .45ACP slug tore through the arm and directly into the chest of the knife wielding killer who fell back against the wall from the impact. At almost the same instant, They heard three shots from a hand gun in the back then the full auto burst of the M-4 as Brad returned fire.

"You shot me Tuck. I can't believe you shot me!" Henry said gritting his teeth against the pain.

Tuck just looked at him and replied, "You'd have done the same for me Henry. Besides, I thought it might be easier to plug a hole in your arm than to sew your head back on."

A low moan sounded from the kitchen and the two moved slowly through the doorway to investigate. Tuck covered the room with the Kimber while Henry fumbled for a light switch with his good hand. A soon as the lights came on, they saw Audrey lying on the floor with a nasty head wound. She was regaining consciousness just as Brad came through the back door, and knelt beside her.

"Bradley, I can't believe it's you," Audrey said in a weak voice, "He was going to kill me, but Henry and Tuck showed up at the front door and interrupted him."

Brad started to respond when gunfire sounded down the hill followed by the crash of metal against metal. As they started to run back through the house, they heard the sound of another crash, and then the sound of a vehicle coming back up the road and into the driveway. Tuck raced through the door just in time to see Hanna drive the battered old jeep up the drive and park. She got out and opened the back door of the jeep to retrieve Emily who was unfazed by all of the action and noise.

"Hanna, are you and Emily all right?" Tuck aske anxiously.

"We're fine Michael, but that agent got shot just after we heard shooting up here. I pushed Lois' car off of the mountain."

"Audrey is hurt Hanna. Can you help her? And Uncle Henry got shot also," He said as he took Emily in one arm and helped steady Hanna with the other.

"Tell her who shot her favorite uncle, Tuck," Henry said still gritting his teeth in pain, "There is a first aid kit under the front seat of the jeep that would probably help me a lot right about now."

"Brad where is the other agent?" Tuck asked.

"He took a couple of rounds in the head as we came around back. Where is the one that was with Hanna?"

"He jumped out of the jeep when Lois turned her lights on, and they shot him," Hanna told him, "Lois didn't get away though. I heard a wolf pack running down below me, and then a really bloodcurdling scream from where the car went down the hill."

"Let's get everybody patched up and wait on Shaun. His team can run sweeper on this op as far as I'm concerned," Brad stated as he comforted his wife.

Fort-five minutes later, Shaun O'Brien arrived with his team and several other local law enforcement personel. He dispatched the ops team to recover Lois' body, if that was possible, and also the shooter that had been crushed by Hanna's counter attack. The deputies bagged the bodies at the house while Shaun debriefed Tuck and Brad. Ten minutes more passed before the EMS arrrived to treat Henry and Julia, and then whisked them away to the Newport Hospital Emergency Room leaving Tuck and Shaun time to talk.

"Shaun, I'm worn out from all of this crap that seems to surround Hanna and me. I'm thinking that we might come down to Honduras and spend a few years off of the grid. What do you think?" Tuck asked.

"Tuck, Honduras is a nasty place to live. There is corruption and poverty everywhere, and unless you are ministering to that, there is not much for a guy like you to do. Even I'm tired of it. Be patient because good things eventually come to those that wait for them," Shaun replied with a smile.

"I hope so. Hanna is still weak from having the baby, and I really worry about how she is holding up," Tuck told him, "I just want to get somewhere quiet so we can have a normal life...whatever that is."

Shaun's team came back to the cabin after securing the remains of Lois Salinas and her men, and they motioned for Shaun to join them.

Just before he turned to go he repeated, "Relax Tuck, everything is going to work out for you and for Hanna."

The ride to the Priest River airport was a quiet one. Hanna just leaned against Tuck who held little Emily against his chest. When they arrived, an FBI security detail ushered them through the small terminal building and into an office where they waited while their plane was readied. Hanna was shivering so Tuck reached over with the arm that wasn't holding the baby and drew her near.

"Michael, this is not the way that I want to raise our little girl, or any of the rest of our children that we are blessed with," Hanna spoke softly to Tuck as he held her close.

"I'm pretty tired of having to be on guard all of the time myself," He replied, "Running to Texas certainly wasn't the solution to our problems that I thought it was going to be. I talked to Shaun a little while ago about maybe going to Honduras, although that is a pretty crappy place to live according to him."

"What did Shaun tell you?" Hanna asked hopefully.

"He just laughed and said that all good things come to them that wait," Tuck answered, "I really don't know what he was talking about. Anyway, Shaun is flying us back to the ranch. Brad and Audrey have already gone with what was left of Lois and her friends, and they didn't think that you would want to be on that flight."

"No, I suppose that would have been a creepy ride. I feel much better returning with you and Emily. How much time do we have?" Hanna asked.

"Henry is coming to the airport as soon as he gets back from being sown up so I'm thinking a couple of hours," Tuck answered.

It had been a long harrowing night, and good people as well as bad had died here, although the quality of the death had to have been better for the agents than for Lois. A bullet was very quick compared to being ripped apart by a pack of ravenous wolves.

Henry Albright came back with his right arm in a sling. The bullet that Tuck had shot through him to kill his would be abductor had nicked the bone and passed through the muscle of the upper arm.

"I'm getting too old for this Tuck. How about finding someplace quiet to settle down so we can visit like regular families do?" Henry asked as he gave Tuck a one arm bear hug at the airport.

"Henry, I don't know what we would do without you. I'm sorry that what seemed like a good idea went so sideways, and that you got hurt because of it," Tuck replied.

"Uncle Henry, I just want you to know that I really love you, and that Daddy would be proud of what you did tonight," Hanna hugged her uncle and kissed him goodbye.

Henry had a big tear starting to come out of his eye so he said with a strained voice, "Yeah, yeah, you guys catch your flight. I need to go home and get a stiff drink."

"We'll call tomorrow and let you know we got back okay," Hanna said, and Tuck shook his hand before they turned to walk into the airport.

Shaun came into the office and ushered them quickly through the terminal and outside to the apron where a Cessna Citation was waiting.

"We'll have to make a stop for fuel about halfway back, so that will be the time for a little leg stretching. I've packed some sandwiches and drinks in that cooler back there. I don't know about you guys, but I'm so hungry, I could eat the rear end of a horse french fried in kerosene!" Shaun exclaimed as he helped Hanna and Emily into the back seat.

"Lovely thought, Shaun. Does that mean that I'm going to be the stewardess on this flight?" Hanna said with a laugh.

"Just send a couple of sandwiches up to Tuck and me after we takeoff," Shaun replied with a grin.

"Aye, aye, Captain Spanky!" Hanna replied with the quip that she used on Tuck when her spirits were high. She was looking forward to a little peace and quiet, and life with Tuck and Emily, and their friends.

Shaun taxied the Cessna unto the runway and soon was airborne, setting its course for their fuel stop in Reno, Nevada.

"Any word from Shaun O'Brien?" John Claiborne asked acting Special Agent Walter Grooms when the man brought him the news that Brad was in the office to debrief.

"No Sir, but it was my understanding that he was re-fueling in Reno before flying on to the ranch," Grooms replied.

"Let me know as soon as you hear from him and ask Brad to come in," Claiborne told him.

"Yes sir," Grooms left the room.

"Brad it's good to see you back and in one piece. I heard that you had a difficult time with Lois Salinas. How is Julia?"

"John, we lost three good agents up there, but managed to save all of the assets. We brought most of Salinas back to autopsy. Julia is fine, but she has a nasty cut on her head and a concussion. Have you heard from Shaun?" Bradley Rumskill finished.

"No word yet, but it is too early to be concerned. They made a fuel stop in Reno, and are probably close to the ranch by now," Claiborne replied, "Why don't you take Julia to the hotel and get some rest. We can do the debriefing tomorrow."

"I think I will. I've got about six years on you, John, and you're too damned old for this type of job!" Brad replied with a laugh as he left the office.

Claiborne sat in the office reflecting on what Brad had just told him. He had served the country through several administrations, and now he felt that it was time to turn in his papers. The change in the political winds boded ill for the country, and John Claiborne was reflecting on those changes when Walter Grooms interrupted his thoughts.

"Yes Agent Grooms, what is it?" Claiborne asked as he looked up at the man.

"We've just received word that a Cessna matching the description of Shaun O'Brien's plane has hit a mountain in New Mexico called Wheeler's Peak. There appears to be no survivors. I'm sorry sir," Grooms told in a broken voice.

"Are they certain that it was his plane?" Claiborne asked as he rose to a standing position, steadying himself with his hands on the desk.

"Search and rescue personnel are on the ground but can't get near the wreckage because the area is very mountainous and remote. They have reported that it also exploded and burned on impact," Grooms reported.

"Get me a Chopper ready immediately. I want to go to the scene and see for myself," Claiborne ordered.

"I already have one standing by sir," Grooms told him as Claiborne started for the door.

"As soon as we have a confirmation, I want you to notify the next of kin. It seems hard to believe that several of the most resilient people that I know would come through what they have in the past few months just to be killed in a simple airplane crash," Claiborne said as he just shook his head in disbelief.

"Yes sir, it does. I'll handle everything here as soon as we get the word," Grooms replied as the director walked out of the door.

CHAPTER 22

Two weeks later in Myrtle Beach, a closed casket ceremony was held in the McMillan Funeral Home Chapel, and then the procession traveled to the Southeastern Memorial Gardens for the internment. John and Louise Post, Mary Moffet pushing Luke in his wheel chair, Bob and Abigail Pike along with Henry, Kathryn Albright, and Hanna's sisters stood with the other mourners as the two caskets were lowered into the ground side by side next to Harry Albright, Hanna's father.

Deputy Isaac Baumgarner stood with several other deputies and men from the South Carolina Department of Natural Resources Including Private Junior Knowles and Colonel McNeery, whose normally stony expression was softened by the tears that flowed unabashedly down his face. Detectives Alvarez Banks and Teddy Loveless stood stoically near the outside of the crowd of friends and family that had gathered to say good-bye to the couple whose lives had touched their hearts.

WLIB Myrtle Beach had a reporter on the scene, but Fox News' Maggie O'Brien, attending her second funeral in as many days, had tears streaming down her cheeks that would have made reporting this event impossible.

Anthony Morris stood with John Claiborne outside of the circle, waiting to add their condolences after the service ended.

"Taking care of the Tuckers' funeral was a good thing for us to do, Director Claiborne," Anthony Morris said quietly, "Tuck would appreciate that you covered travel expenses for his friends."

"Call me John, Anthony. I felt like it was something that we owed him after all that the government put him and his family through. I'm leaving right after the funeral, and I wanted to tell you that paperwork has been submitted for your next promotion and transfer, if you want it," Claiborne told him.

"This is a surprise John. I'm honored," Morris answered.

"I've decided to retire effectively immediately, Anthony. This young man's death taught me a valuable lesson about the brevity of life, and I'm not wasting anymore of mine. You'll be moving into bigger circles if you decide to make the move, just watch your six," Claiborne explained.

"I will John and thank you again," Special Agent Morris replied with a handshake as the service ended, and the crowd started gathering around the family to offer condolences.

Brad and Audrey Rumskill were back on Thunder Ranch when the funerals for Shaun O'Brien and the Tucker family were held in Myrtle Beach, South Carolina. Audrey was still suffering from vertigo as a result of the blow that she had taken, and the doctors had advised against flying.

"Brad, why don't we take a little ride around the ranch today?" Audrey asked, "I think that it will help lift both of our spirits."

"If you think that you are up to it dear. I know just the place where I would like to go," Brad answered with a smile.

He helped her into one of the Polaris Rangers, and they drove to the pond where Tuck had found the monkey. Brad had been driving out and leaving fruit for the little guy every day for the past two weeks, but the monkey wouldn't come near him. Maybe today would be different.

He parked the ATV away from the edge of the pond while Audrey got the bag of fruit that he kept in the back. As she turned toward the live oak tree that the monkey called home, she was surprised to see him on the ground and running toward her. He threw himself on Audrey and clung to her with his arms around her neck.

She slowly walked back to the ATV and got in, "Let's drive back to the house, Brad. I think the monkey wants to come home."

The monkey rode the whole way back with his arms locked around Audrey's neck, and making little chirping sounds. When they arrived at the house, he saw the white wolf in the pen near the side door and jumped to the ground. In a flash he was in the pen and on the back of the wolf who tolerated his antics.

"It looks like they might have known each other," Brad observed with a smile, "Tuck would have been glad that we got him back here before the weather got ugly."

"It was so sad to lose them like that, just when everything else had worked out. What a nice young couple, and it breaks my heart that they died so young, and little Emily..," Audrey said, her voice breaking so that she didn't finish her thought.

"It is difficult to accept, but I think about them also, and losing O'Brien after getting through this trouble together just seems so surreal," Brad told her, "On a lighter note, we have to make a decision about our names this week or we'll have to take care of a lot of paperwork to undo the last twenty years as Otis and Julia."

"I'm hanging on to Julia, you can do what you want. Besides, how are you going to tell that story about the witness protection deal?" Audrey told him.

"You're right. It will be much easier to keep our fake names instead of changing to our real ones. I guess Otis will have to do," Brad told her in surrender.

"We've just saved tons of money and hours of hassles with our attorney and paperwork, let's celebrate! The hands had that bull that Tuck killed hanging in the cooler while they butchered it. I'll bet I can find a steak somewhere in there with our name on it," She said with a laugh while wiping the tears from her eyes.

"I'll get a fire going and open a bottle of wine while you get the meat. Maybe we can watch the sunset this afternoon like we used to," Otis said with a big smile.

"Whatever your name is, you haven't changed a bit, Otis Jamieson!' Julia exclaimed with a big smile, "Still the romantic that I fell in love with."

Then on a more somber note, "I wonder if Hanna and Tuck would have turned out like us if they had lived. You know what I mean, good friends with each other."

"I believe they would have. After everything they went through, the marriage had to be blessed to hold up for the short time that it did," Otis replied thoughtfully.

Julia just shook her head in agreement as she left to cut the steak.

EPILOGUE

The secluded marina sat back from the ocean several blocks, and was home to several charter boats ranging in size from several twenty foot center console craft, an older but pristine 28 foot Chris Craft, a thirty one foot blue Bahia Mar Bertram that was outfitted with a half tower and tournament outriggers, an older 42 foot Rybovich with a full tower and all of the detail that the maker was known for, and at the end of the dock, a beautiful old 42 foot Bertram in full fighting trim. She sported a full Pipe Welder's tower, tournament outriggers that had been rigged for several lines per side, and a beautiful, hand fitted walnut fighting chair in the cockpit.

"Ahoy the Sandpiper!" the tall, heavyset older man called out as he neared the stern of the Bertram. A darkly tanned young man stuck his head out of the salon and answered, "Hello sir, can I help you?"

"Does this vessel belong to George and Stephanie Alexander?" he asked.

"Yes, but they're ashore right now stocking up for tomorrow's charter. I'm just helping get things organized," The young man replied, "If you want to wait on them, it shouldn't be more than thirty minutes before they get back."

"That's all right. Just tell them a prospective client stopped by to look at the boat. I'll be in touch," He answered with a smile as he turned and walked back down the dock.

He sat across the busy parking lot from the ramp, slumped in the seat of his rental car and waited. Thirty minutes later an old jeep drove up and a tall, sun bronzed young man got out with his very pregnant and equally sun tanned wife, followed by a two-year-old girl that they swung playfully between them as they walked down the marina ramp to their boat.

Henry Albright watched until they were onboard, and then started the car. With a smile on his face, he drove out of the parking lot and headed towards the Barbados airport feeling very satisfied with his handiwork.

The End

Acknowledgements

Once again, my heartfelt thanks to all of my friends and family members that contributed to this endeavor. I especially want to thank Delmer and Jane McAfee for their hospitality on the beautiful Smokey Mountain Ranch, which was the inspiration for the Thunder Ranch setting.

I also want to thank Kevin Zimdars and Vincent Lavallee for taking the time to share their experiences about patrolling the border regions of Texas, and especially Kevin for sharing some pastoral wisdom which I managed to work into the story.

Thanks to David Dinkela of All American Firearms Service for encouraging me in my writing and for giving me a venue to meet some great storytellers.

Thanks to my good friend Tom Stewart for sharing his knowledge of the country, Chacho Gonzales, a good friend and story teller, and my dear friends at The West Texas Cowboy Church, especially Pastor Andy, Lori, Lou Etta, George, Travis, Maxine, and the entire congregation for welcoming us when we were able to visit.

God Bless Texas!

Other Books by W.W. Brock:

COUGAR!
NIGHT WIND

CPSIA information can be obtained
at www.ICGtesting.com
Printed in the USA
FFOW03n2129150716
25805FF